LITTLE RED RIDING SLUT: TAMING THE BEAST

RILEY ROSE

BOOK TWO IN THE LITTLE RED RIDING SLUT SERIES

Copyright © 2024 Riley Rose

Cover Design by Kingofdesigner on Fiverr

All rights reserved. No part of this publication may be reproduced, distributed, or transmitted in any form or by any means without the the prior written permission of the author, except in the case of brief quotations for review purposes.

This is a work of fiction and any resemblance to real people, places, or situations is coincidental.

Originally published on Kindle Vella as Little Red Riding Slut: Episodes 16-34

Read all the Episodes of Little Red Riding Slut on Kindle Vella

Read Episodes 1-15 in Book 1 - Little Red Riding Slut: Fairytale Fantasy

Sign-Up for my E-Mail List to Stay Up-To-Date on New Releases!

Visit RileyRoseErotica.com for more sexy stories!

Chapter 1

Red woke with a big cock in her face. So she already knew it would be a good morning.

She instantly recognized it as Harry's. She knew his headless monster anywhere.

She was in a cushy bed, inverted to Harry, her face by his crotch rather than his chest.

So she did what any good slut would upon finding a juicy penis inches away. She shoved it in her mouth and got to sucking.

It grew within her, filling her oral orifice and tickling the back of her throat.

She slurped him up good, loving how he throbbed between her lips and anticipating the sticky gift he was about to give her.

His hips twitched. His cock pulsated inside her mouth. And then he blew his load straight down her throat.

She sucked him hard, pumping him for every last drop. She didn't want one ounce to go anywhere but inside her. She closed her eyes and enjoyed his creamy goodness coating her throat.

"Ohhhh my goodness!" he moaned. "What a way to wake

up!"

Red released his flaccid penis and gazed up at him. Oops, he had been asleep that whole time? Oh well, he certainly didn't seem to mind.

"Red!" Celestine chastised on the other side of her. Apparently, the three of them had shared the same bed. That was a good way to save money and was super-cozy. "Are you hogging Harry's dick again?"

"Sorry! Here, I'll share his cum with you." She plastered her lips to Celestine and kissed her, sloshing the yummy cum that was still in her mouth into the witch's.

Celestine cooed contentedly, enjoying both Red's kiss and the taste of their headless lover.

Harry got hard from watching the two beautiful women make out and share his seed.

Red and Celestine both grabbed his shaft, jerking him off while they continued to kiss. He erupted before long, splattering their hips and thighs.

"Better?" Red asked.

"Much," the kinky witch replied. "But I expect you to do more to thank me for healing you from all your tree fucking."

"You did?" Red realized her pussy and ass were nowhere near as sore as they should be after being impaled by a ridiculous number of huge vines. Celestine must have used her magic to heal Red while she slept.

She threw her arms around her new friend. "Thank you so much! You're the best sexy witch I've ever met."

"It was my pleasure," Celestine replied with a smile. "But

you need one last treatment."

"Okay!" Red loved treatments from beautiful witches.

"Lay back."

Red complied, plopping onto the pillow. Harry's head was on the fluffy cushion next to her. His nude, muscular body pressed against her. Celestine curled up on the other side.

The witch flicked her wand along Red's pussy, making the young slut instantly wet. Then she pierced Red's barrier and slid the wand in as far as it would go, the wooden handle jutting out from Red's moist lips.

"Uhhhhhhhh!" Red moaned. "F... fucking your wand is going to heal me?"

"Yes. Just leave it inside your pussy and let it work its magic."

"O... okay." Red squirmed in the sheets, the magic making it feel like there were sexy ants crawling inside her.

"I very much enjoy what your magic is doing to her," Harry said.

"Yes, she looks like quite the helpless slut, doesn't she?"

"Hey!" Red protested. "Oh wait, I love being a helpless slut." She shimmied, unable to keep her hips from jumping all over the place. "B... but I can't control my body with what your wand is doing to me."

Celestine patted the younger woman's thigh. "I know, it's quite overwhelming. But I promise it will take away all your soreness when it's finished."

"Ohhhhhhhh!" Red replied, her butt leaping off the bed from the magical pulses shooting through her tender vagina.

The wand was driving her absolutely wild.

"Harry, shove your cock in her mouth," Celestine instructed. "That will keep her preoccupied."

"But what about y… mmrph!" Red's question was cut off by the fleshy sword once again filling her mouth. It was amazing how quickly Harry could resume his erection after spilling his seed. It meant Red and Celestine could feel his hard shaft in their mouths, pussies, and asses anytime they wanted.

"Don't worry about me, my young slut," the witch informed her. "I'll keep busy by probing your tight ass." She rolled Red onto her side and shoved a magic finger in her companion's butt.

Red groaned into Harry's cock. Magic fingers were the best. Especially when they were in her ass.

She whimpered as she sucked the headless salami and got a deep anal exam. Celestine vibrated her finger, making Red's ass throb with a burning desire to be fucked long and hard.

The wand was still wreaking blissful havoc between her thighs, her lovers preventing her trembling body from doing too many gymnastics.

She surrendered to the triple probing, letting her friends have their way with her.

The wand built up the orgasmic feelings inside her until she came. But it wasn't like a normal orgasm. It was like some heavenly power coursed through her, curing her pussy of any fatigue while simultaneously making it feel like she was cumming. But without any of the usual squirting. A non-cumming orgasm. Different. Strange. Amazing!

Celestine worked similar healing magic on Red's ass. And while Harry couldn't do magic, his cum flowing down her throat had its own healing properties, making her feel warm and cozy and like her usual slutty self.

When her holes were free, she melted into the bed, feeling completely at peace. "Ohhh wow, that was amazing. I feel so rested."

"Good," Celestine said. "The magic worked well on your naughty parts."

Red smiled. "Thank you both for taking care of me. I really appreciate it. And will show that appreciation by fucking you non-stop and being your fuck toy whenever you want!"

Harry grinned. "You are a most accommodating young woman."

"And an excellent fuck toy," Celestine added.

"You know it!" Red agreed. "But before I become a fuck toy, we need to take care of Harry's problem."

"You mean his non-stop erection?" the witch asked.

"No, silly! His headless head."

"Oh, yes." Celestine looked away, frowning.

Red pinched her butt. "Hey! You promised to help him."

"I do want to help him. It's just... I don't have the power to remove the curse."

"What?!" Red and Harry exclaimed.

Red sat up. "But you're the one who put the curse on him?"

"Yes, but just because I bestowed the curse doesn't mean I

can remove it."

"That doesn't make any sense."

"Magic doesn't always make sense."

"Magic is stupid!"

"Might I remind you my magic has given you multiple mind-blowing orgasms."

"Oh, right. Well, that magic is great. Curse magic is stupid."

"It is fraught with difficulties," the witch agreed. "I was young and cast a curse I hadn't mastered. That is why I cannot dispel it."

Red shook the kooky witch. Mainly to knock some sense into her. A nice side effect was watching big witch tits sway back and forth. "Celestine! Stop doing sneaky magic you don't understand!"

"I don't do it anymore. Well, not as often anyway."

"You're incorrigible."

"Well, you're an incorrigible slut."

"Hey, we're both incorrigible sluts!"

Harry leaped between them, his cock separating their nude bodies. "Is there anyone who can remove the curse?"

Celestine nodded. "There's a magical rose kept high up in a castle in Avinnois that supposedly can cure any curse."

Red bounced on the bed. "Great! Let's get it!"

"Not so fast my impetuous young friend," the witch replied, putting the kibosh on Red's bouncing. "The master of the castle never allows anyone entry unless they are a young woman just out of maidenhood."

Red bounced again. "I'm a young woman just out of maidenhood!"

"A woman who is willing to be truly slutty," Celestine continued.

"I'm truly slutty!"

"And be willing to be treated like a complete sex toy."

"I love being a sex toy!"

Celestine tapped her finger to her lips, surveying Red's nude body. "Hmm, I guess you are perfect for this job."

"Yes!" Red clasped her hands together, excited she met all the slutty requirements.

"But what of the castle owner?" Harry inquired. "He could be a fiend who would kidnap Red."

"I know nothing of his sense of chivalry or even what he looks like," Celestine answered. "All I know is people say he's a real beast in the bedroom."

Red shivered. "I love beasts. Especially in the bedroom."

She snatched Harry's cock, which immediately stood at attention. "I'll get that rose for you and get your head back on your sexy body."

"Egads, Red I can't think straight while you're stroking my manhood."

"Why do you think I'm doing it?" she replied, pumping his shaft hard. "This way you can't argue with me about going."

"Who said I was going to… ahhhhhhhh!" His eyes rolled back in his head as Red's fingers roamed up to the tip of his dick. She massaged his bulbous head around its opening.

"You were going to say it's too dangerous and I can't go alone. And I was going to remind you I'm a skilled monster hunter and can handle myself. Especially when it comes to people who are super-horny!"

"That's true," Celestine remarked. "I don't think there is anyone who can resist Red's natural charms."

"Aw, Celestine." Red yanked the witch into a hug with one hand while the other continued to stroke Harry's trembling cock.

"F… fine," the headless warrior said. "You may go alone. On one condition."

"What's that?"

"You finish jerking me off until I come all over you and Celestine."

"Gladly!" Red pumped him hard. Celestine joined the fun, and they had him gushing in no time, aiming his cock so his seed sprayed across their tits.

Then they took turns sucking him off until he coated their faces in his warm juice. That made him so relaxed he would have agreed to anything they wanted.

Celestine helped Red into her crimson bra and panties while Harry fastened her cloak around her shoulders.

She snatched her sword and kissed both of them on the lips. "I'll be back before you know it. Don't have too much kinky fun while I'm gone."

"I can't promise that," Celestine replied, eying the headless cock. "Harry and I have a lot of catching up to do."

"Aw, c'mon," Red whined. "You're going to suck up all his

cum and leave nothing for me, you little witch slut."

Celestine raised her eyebrows and smirked, indicating that was exactly what she was going to do. Stupid sexy witch.

Harry brushed Red's hair behind her ear. "Do not worry, Red. I will give you vigorous fuckings all day long when you return and will pleasure you as much as you want."

She leaped into Harry's arms. She would have kissed him again, but his head was resting on the bed.

"As will I," Celestine said, pressing her naked breasts against Red's back and fondling the young woman's butt. Okay, maybe she wasn't such a stupid witch after all.

"You guys really know how to motivate a girl! I'm off!"

Her cloak fluttered out as she twirled toward the door, giving them one last glimpse of her thong-clad ass.

Then she barreled down the stairs of the inn, eager to tame a horny beast.

Chapter 2

Red caught a ride on a wagon with a cute farm lass. They took a roll in the hay during the journey. A literal roll in the hay as that's what the girl was transporting.

She bid her companion adieu just before Grancia, letting the golden-tressed lass fondle her butt one last time.

Red knew a shortcut to Avinnois through The Whispering Woods. The forest was frequented by bandits, scary creatures, and ghosts. But it would take a full day off her journey, and Red was determined to get that rose for Harry as soon as possible.

She kept her hand on the hilt of her sword as she traversed the woods. It was too bad it was known to be so dangerous. It was quite lovely, with birds flitting about and cute critters scampering across her boots.

Just when she was beginning to think she'd have an uneventful evergreen traipse, she heard shrieks up ahead. Very annoying shrieks.

She hurried through the brush until she emerged into a clearing. Where she was treated to quite a sight.

Six goblins were frantically trying to avoid the tongue of a tusked toad. It looked like a normal toad except fifty times the size and a hundred times more frightening. It had large, sharp tusks jutting from either side of its slimy mouth.

And these weren't just any goblins. They were the ones who gave Red a crazy butt fucking just a couple of days ago. One of Red's rules was she had to save anyone who gave her an amazing fucking in her rear end. So she had to come to these goblins' aid.

Red dashed into the fray, her silver sword gleaming as it came free of its scabbard. "Hey, you horny toad! Scantily clad girl over here." She wasn't sure if tusked toads found humans attractive, but shouting and shaking her tits should at least get its attention.

It did. It also got the attention of the goblins. They halted their screaming antics, drooling over Red's exposed flesh.

"It iz human female wit de hottest ass," the goblin leader remarked.

"Yup, that's me, Miss Hot Ass." Red leaped to the side and rolled along the ground, barely avoiding the toad's tongue attack. "Let me take care of toady here, and you can ogle my booty all you want."

"We love te ogle yer booty," another goblin replied. The six of them giddily rushed to the tree line, where they could safely watch the battle and hungrily ogle Red's butt.

Red flitted across tree stumps and branches, acrobatically avoiding the long, slimy tongue and looking for an opening to close the distance between her and her adversary.

She jumped straight up, splitting her legs, so the next strike passed between them, the toad's saliva almost touching her skimpy panties. With a tongue like that, this toad could probably perform some serious cunnilingus. But there were some creatures even Red couldn't bring herself to fuck. Though that was a pretty short list.

The tongue retracted just as her feet hit the ground. It snaked around her ankles and upended her.

She landed on her back, her sword tumbling from her hand.

The toad dragged her along the grass, the ground loosening the strings of her bikini top. It was whisked off, leaving her bare breasts to jiggle as her butt bounced along the ground.

"Me like dis toad," a goblin remarked.

"Ya, it good at stripping sluts," another added.

"Take off all slut's clothes!" a third cried.

"You're not helping!" Red yelled back. "Can you give me a hand?"

"Nah," the leader replied. "We rather see it rip yer panties off."

Red sighed. Goblins were very annoying. But she had to do something. The toad continued to reel her in. She usually loved a good tongue lashing, but not from gross amphibians. And this toad was gross: it had huge eyes that bulged out of its head, brown pock-marked skin, and breath so rancid Red thought it would melt the rest of her clothes.

She flailed her arms along the ground, frantically searching for any kind of natural weapon. Her fingers closed around a rock the size of an ogre's balls. She grabbed it with both hands and smashed it down on the toad's tongue.

It made a disgusting retching sound, releasing Red and whipping its tongue back into its mouth.

She sprang to her feet and made a beeline for her blade.

The toad's tongue shot out again, striking Red in the ass like a wet, slimy spanking.

"Eek!" she yelped. The coarse texture of the tongue was a weird sensation. Though not an entirely unpleasant one. Guess she really was an ass slut if even ugly toads spanking her turned her on.

The goblins cheered from the sidelines. "Yah, spank dat slut!"

"You guys are still not helping!" she replied, zigzagging away from the hopping toad and getting a few more slimy spankings.

"We help after yer naked," the head gobby said. Oh great, they probably wanted to fuck her again. Actually, that was great. Goblins were weird, but they did give her a good ass ramming. She wouldn't mind taking some goblin cock in her tight, little butt again.

The toad hopped forward, one giant leap bringing it right behind Red. She ran up the trunk of a tree and propelled herself off it. She flipped backwards, soaring over the toad before landing on its head.

She whisked her cloak off and draped it across the creature's eyes.

The toad leaped around erratically, trying to dislodge the annoying human atop it. Red's breasts bounced every which way, much to the delight of the goblins.

"Dis is good titty show," one of the goblins said.

"Ya, shake her boobies harder," another requested.

The toad complied, hopping like it had hot coals on its webbed feet, making Red put on an even bouncier titty show.

"Would you guys do something useful?" Red yelled at her oglers.

"We be very useful," the leader replied. "We growing our cocks real big." That was true. All six of them had sprung such large erections their loincloths had popped off.

Red stared at their quivering cocks, thinking about what she wanted to do to them. These goblins were useless in a fight but did know how to use their big dicks.

Before she could enjoy those dicks, she needed to dispatch the toad. The scaly creature continued to hop blindly until one particularly huge leap sent it straight for a tree.

"Oh shi… ahhhhhhh!" Red's curse was cut off as the toad rammed face first into the trunk. She flew forward, smacked into a branch, and fell.

Her panties snagged the toad's tusk and got pulled down. She found herself upside down, suspended from the tusk with her thong around her knees.

Fortunately, the toad had knocked itself out. Unfortunately, six goblins leered at her inverted, nude body, their cocks bobbing in eager anticipation.

"Wow, yer fierce warrior," the main goblin told her.

"Ya, ye showed toad who boss," another cheered.

"Oh, thanks. But, um, could you guys help me down?"

"Nah, we rather watch yer tits and ass."

Just as Red was thinking that goblins were the most annoying creatures ever, she slipped out of her panties and thudded to the forest floor.

The head goblin twirled his dick around. "Ah good, now yer ready to be fucked."

Red had fallen with her ass sticking up, the favorite target for goblin cocks. She flipped over, shoving her finger in his big-nosed face. "Okay, listen up, goblins. I just saved you from being eaten by this toad. You should show some gratitude."

They scratched their green heads, a few stray hairs sprouting out of each one at weird angles.

"What iz grabibude?" one asked. Goblins didn't possess a large vocabulary.

"It means to show thanks," Red informed them.

They nodded in understanding. "We show grabibude by fucking you in tight ass."

Red rolled her eyes. Of course, that's how they would show their appreciation. "Not this time, gobbies. I want you guys to lick my pussy. It's the least you can do for saving your lives."

"Aww, but we like yer ass."

She grabbed the leader by the scruff of his shirt. "Listen up, my pussy is super-tight and cute and deserves to be fucked, got it?" Red wasn't usually so forceful with her sex requests, but these goblins needed to learn how to pleasure a woman in more places than her butt.

"Okay, okay. Sheesh, yer touchy."

"No, I want to be touched. By your goblin tongues. So get to licking, boys!" She spread her legs, revealing her glistening, bare pussy.

That got them more excited about the task. They wrestled over who would get to go first, cursing each other and uttering various explicit things about her vagina.

Red sighed. Goblins were the silliest creatures she had ever encountered.

"Guys!" she yelled, interrupting their shenanigans. "Just do it in the same order as last time."

"Good idea," the main goblin replied. "Yer smart lady."

"Me also horny lady." Oh great, now she was talking like them. "Please lick my pussy and make me cum!"

"Yah, me lick human pussy real good." He dove between her legs and slobbered her with his tongue. He was nowhere near as skilled as Harry or Celestine, but his tongue was long and had ridges that felt very nice along Red's lips.

"Mm, dis tasty pussy."

"Th… thanks," Red cooed. "Wanna see how it tastes inside?"

"Yah, yah." He pierced her barrier. The coarseness of his tongue made her gasp. It was thicker than a human's and filled her pleasantly, its ridges massaging her tender walls.

Red threw her head back and let out a long, low sigh. It was so nice having something squishy in her pussy. What the goblin lacked in skill he made up for in length, his tongue reaching all the way to her cervix. He tickled it, making her squirm along the ground.

The other goblins gathered around, stroking their cocks as they eagerly watched her gyrations. Red knew she was going to get five streams of gobby juice all over her. And just when she had finally been cum-free for more than a few minutes. Ah, what the heck. As long as they made her climax, she was fine with them spreading their gloppy gift on her.

"Me love noises human girls make," one cock-stroker said.

"Specially dis girl," another remarked.

"Yah, she real slut," a third opined.

"Hey!" Red complained. "Do you really need to comment on every slutty thing I do?"

They glanced at each other, then back at her. "Yep."

"Oh. Okay! It's really turning me on." Being called a slut made her wetter and more likely to have epic orgasms.

They called her a bunch of other whorish things while their leader tongue fucked her hard. Her probed every part of her until he had her writhing so hard she was pulling out swatches of grass.

"Ohhhhhh, y… you're going to make me cum!" she wailed.

"Cum slut! Cum slut! Cum slut!" the other goblins chanted.

Red came like a cum slut. She splattered the goblin's face, her back arching off the earth while screams ripped form her throat.

"Ohhhhhhhhhh fuuuuuucckkkkkk!"

That set off all five goblins circled around her. They ejaculated at the same time, dumping their seed across her tits, stomach, thighs, and face.

Which just made her climax even harder. The head gobby pulled out and lapped up her leaky faucet. His tongue was both pleasurable and ticklish. She could get used to goblins going down on her.

She finished her spillage while the goblins shot the remainder of their thick sauce across her nude body.

Then they yanked her boots off and bent her legs up on either side of her so her feet were up by her head. Thank goodness Red was so flexible. It allowed for very kinky sex positions.

The second goblin went tongue diving, taking advantage of the perfect position Red's pussy was in with her ankles up by her ears.

"Yer pussy real tasty," the head goblin said, smacking his lips and stroking his cock near her face.

"Uhhhhh, th… thanks," she replied, enjoying his friend's long appendage worming into her. "Y… you have a good tongue for fucking pussies."

"Yah. Goblin tongues de best."

The tongue-licking goblin's mates cheered him on as he made Red moan and her knees tremble.

"Ohhhh yes!" she cried. "Tongue fuck my slutty pussy! Shove it all the way into me!"

He shoved it all the way into her, twirling his tongue in different ways than the first goblin. Red loved experiencing a variety of tongue twisters, particularly ones inside her wet pussy.

She gave that goblin a nice facial then did the same for the third after he bent her over and licked her lips while planting his face in her ass.

The fourth gobster lifted her onto his shoulders with her thighs wrapped around his head and her pussy plastered to his mouth. He held her up while slithering inside her.

Red forgot goblins were quite strong, especially for their small stature. The fact that this goblin could keep her in the air while pleasuring her made her hot as hell.

She fought to keep her balance as she wiggled on top of him. She gushed spectacularly down his throat, showing him how much she appreciated his manliness, or gobliness.

The last two to go were the brothers. The other four held Red's arms and legs, spread-eagling her and letting the siblings have their way with her.

They both shoved their tongues inside her at the same time, just like they had simultaneously rammed their cocks inside her ass at their last meeting.

"Ohhhhhhhhh," she whimpered. "D… do you guys do everything together?"

"Yep," replied one brother.

"Iz dat strange?" asked the other.

"N… no, it's great. Please keep doing it. I feel so full with both your tongues inside me."

"Yah, let's fill slut real good."

"Me favorite thing to do!"

They got back to work. Red squirmed helplessly, held down by their brethren. She loved being powerless while these goblins stuck their slimy tongues inside her. She loved that six different varieties of saliva were inside her and that each goblin had made her spill her secret sauce.

"Ye like the way we restrain you?" the leader asked.

"Fuck! I love it!"

"I tink it make ye even bigger slut."

"Yes! Anytime I'm bound and fucked, I become the biggest slut in the land!" Maybe Red shouldn't have confessed all her slutty secrets to them, but she was craving goblin cock. The more they pleasured her, the more she wanted to keep fucking them. And let them fuck her in all her tight holes.

The brothers kept exploring her cavern. It was overwhelming having two tongues so deep inside her, jockeying to find the spots that made her squeal the most. She couldn't stop moaning, couldn't stop wishing these goblin tongues would take up permanent residence in her slutty center.

The one switched to her clit, flicking his thick tongue along it, while the other continued thrusting into her.

"I love being fucked by brothers!" she screamed just before the hugest climax yet ripped out of her. Red had fucked a few brothers, and sisters, during her sexual exploits. Many competed with their siblings to see who could make her cum the hardest. And these goblin brothers proved no different.

They fought with each other to see who could lap up the most pussy juice. Red writhed and squirted and told them she wanted to be a goblin fuck toy for eternity. That made them all very happy.

After her final orgasm subsided, she lay panting on the grass, gazing up at them.

"Ye like pussy licking we do?" the main goblin asked.

"Oh yes. It… it was wonderful."

"Great. Now we fuck ye in ass."

"What?"

"C'mon, we deserve it after making ye spill lady juice."

"Well, you were pretty good at that. But I want to be fucked in more than just my ass."

"No problem. We fuck ye in pussy and mouth and then ass. Sound good?"

Red envisioned the goblins on top of her, shoving their cocks down her throat and deep in her pussy.

"Sounds great!"

It was time to be a goblin fuck toy for the second time.

Chapter 3

Red lay on her back, enjoying the big goblin cock in her mouth and the even bigger one in her pussy.

Her wrists and ankles were tied to the ground with vines, her limbs outstretched and making her look very helpless. Actually, she was helpless. All she could do was wiggle around while she got a dual goblin fucking.

The goblin leader smashed his cock hard into her wet pussy while another goblin squatted over her and face fucked her.

They had done such a good job licking her pussy she had promised them they could fuck all her other holes. And she always kept sexual promises.

"Oo, Chief, ye really stuffing her pussy," a goblin remarked as he stroked his cock.

"Yah, and she real greedy about sucking cock," another commented.

The mouth fucker groaned in delight. "Ohhhh, yah, she best cock sucker ever!" He shoved his goblin dick farther down Red's throat.

"Mhrmph!" Red gasped, unable to form words with a juicy cock in her mouth. These goblins loved describing what a slut she was. They totally got her! Red always got more turned on when her partners called her dirty names. And she definitely didn't mind being awarded the title of best blowjob performer. Now she really was going to suck this gobby off and gulp down all his thick cum.

She dutifully blew him as he thrust harder into her mouth. At the same time, the leader was pounding her pussy for all it was worth. Red hoped it was worth a lot. She took great pride in her cute cooch.

She could hear the tusked toad snoring nearby. Hopefully, it would stay snoozing during the goblin gang bang. She was in a precarious position to fight if it woke up. But she couldn't refuse the goblins' offer to bind her. Being a bound slut was her thing!

"Uhhhhh!" the goblin commander moaned. "Human pussy so tight!"

"Mouth nice and tight too!" his comrade echoed. "Me cum down it real soon. Give her good taste of goblin seed."

"Yah, me fill pussy good. So much she overflow with goblin sauce."

Red moaned into the cock as her body thrashed. They were talking about her like she was nothing but a fuck toy for them to deposit their cum in. Goddess, that was so fucking hot! She would absolutely be their goblin fuck toy.

The two goblins went even harder until they groaned in their unpleasant, guttural goblin way and shot their sticky seed into her. She squealed loudly as their viscous liquid flowed down her throat and up her tight cavern. Even though goblins looked gross, their cum tasted pretty good. Red closed her eyes and gulped down the gobby gift and bucked her hips, gladly accepting the deposit in her pussy.

"Ahhhhh!" the one fucking her mouth moaned. "She such big slut she suck me dry."

The leader continued to shoot spurt after spurt between her legs. "Yah, and her pussy keep squeezing me cock so I can't stop cumming."

Red couldn't respond, but it was true. Her pussy had a vice grip on his girthy goblinhood, milking it for its creamy substance. And she greedily was sucking the slightly smaller dick in her mouth, drinking him up like he was spewing sweet milk down her throat.

The chief goblin rubbed her clit as he continued to fuck her and had her cumming in no time. She shrieked into the cock in her mouth and squirted past the one in her pussy. She was glad to see the goblins were taking her pleasure into account as well as their own. Maybe goblins could learn something after all.

As soon as her goblin lovers pulled out, two more stepped in to take their place, giving her mouth and pussy barely a moment of rest. She was helpless to protest. And, quite frankly, didn't want to. She had committed to being a goblin slut, so she was going to do her best to whore herself out.

The other goblins played with her tits and clit. Rough hands fondled her large breasts, and ridged tongues flicked along her nipples and clit.

Red convulsed on the ground, loving what the goblins were doing to her. The coarseness of their tongues stimulated her sensitive spots more than she was used to. Goblins were becoming one of her favorite creatures!

The two fucking her pussy and mouth unloaded, so she now had two different flavors in her cunt and two coating her throat. And she knew she was far from done with being their plaything.

The brothers were the last ones, and true to form, they wanted the same hole.

Red's jaw dropped as she saw their two dicks head for her mouth. "Hey, wait, one at a ti… mrmphhh!" While she was speaking, the goblin brothers shoved both their cocks past her lips. They were smaller than their brethren, but taking two at once was still an overload.

They alternated thrusting fully into her throat, which made it easier to take, but having two goblin dicks on her lips still made her feel like the biggest whore in the forest.

The four remaining goblins liked the brothers' idea. They took turns shoving their cocks into her pussy. One fat dick would slide in and out of her, followed by a second goblin cock, a third, and a fourth. They kept this rotation going while the brothers continued dominating her mouth.

Red wasn't used to so many different cocks slipping in and out of her so quickly. It made her feel like she was the town whore, tied up in the center square with everyone taking their turn fucking her captive pussy. That thought made her incredibly wet. As did the fact that these goblins were using her body as they saw fit. She hadn't realized how skilled they were in turning human women into goblin sluts.

The two brothers came at the same time, dumping their sticky semen down her throat.

While they were doing that, the four other goblins came inside her pussy in quick succession. Red felt like there was a never-ending stream of cum flowing into her. She wormed around on the ground, barely able to take it but not wanting it to stop.

She swallowed all the brothers' gift like a good girl, and, as a reward, they dripped the remaining post-cum on her face.

When the other four finished with her pussy, four flavors of cum poured out of her. They had filled her to capacity, where she couldn't keep all their juices in.

She panted on the ground, tied up and covered in cum, with six goblins staring down at her.

"How ye feel now?" the leader asked.

"L… like a total goblin slut," she replied.

"Great! We do gud job, lads." The other goblins celebrated with the leader, doing strange goblin handshakes and even stranger goblin dances.

Red rolled her eyes. Is this how they celebrated after turning a girl into their sex toy? "Can you goblins untie me now?"

"Nah," the head gobby told her. "We like sluts tied up."

"But Chief," another goblin said. "We need to untie her to git her in gud position to fuck ass."

"Oh, right. Yer real smart." The main gobster led his minions in quickly freeing Red and then flipping her onto her hands and knees, so her butt was in prime fucking position.

Red trembled, goblin cum still leaking out of her pussy. "D... do you have to fuck me in the ass again?"

"Yah yah yah!" All six of them yelled.

"It our favorite ting te do," the leader added. "Plus, you promise."

Red sighed. She did promise they could fuck her in her tight little hole. It's not that she didn't want them to. It just would have been nice to get a break after guzzling down so much cum and having her pussy flooded with it. But she supposed her ass was the one hole that had room for sticky sauce. So she might as well have that filled with goblin cum too.

"Okay, go ahead," she said with more enthusiasm, remembering how their cocks felt in her tiny cavern last time.

They took turns ass fucking her, one after the other. And then went another round after they were all done. She got so exhausted, she collapsed onto her stomach. She let them lift her hips up and continue to probe her tight butt while she moaned into the grass.

She was very glad the tusked toad was such a heavy sleeper. Her loud moans would have surely woken any other creature.

She now had just as much cum dripping out of her ass as her pussy, maybe even more.

"Ohhhh fuck, I'm such an ass slut!!" she screamed.

"We love ass sluts!" The six goblins yelled.

"Fuck me hard! Fill me with all your sticky, goblin sauce!" That really motivated them to ram her ass. She knew she was going to be very sore after this, but she didn't care. She was getting such epic anal right now, all she could think about was how much her ass belonged to these goblins.

They had one last trick in store for her after each of them went two rounds with her ass.

All six of them decided to fuck her at once.

Two of them lay underneath her, resting her back against their chests. Then, they shoved both their cocks up her ass.

Three others spread her legs and came in from the top, entering her pussy at different angles.

And the leader, who had the biggest dick, shoved his cock down her throat.

Red couldn't even describe the sensations she was feeling. She had three goblin cocks in her pussy, two in her ass, and one in her mouth. Never in her slut-filled life had she been this full, this on the verge of being overloaded with yummy creature cocks. She had no idea how she was fitting them all inside her. But she did know she had reached a new level of slutdom. She had become an epic whore, one who could rival the biggest sluts out there. It was something to be proud of. She would have to tell Harry and Celestine all about it in great detail when she got back.

All six of them fucked her at once. She couldn't scream, couldn't think straight, couldn't do anything except surrender herself to the goblins. She had never been fucked by so many creatures at once. Never had this many cocks filling her tiny holes. She felt completely subservient, like her official title was Receiver of Goblin Cum. Like Receiver of Taxes, but way more sticky.

She literally couldn't process any information beside the six thick cocks thrusting in and out of her. Her whole world became cocks. Cocks in her pussy, cocks in her mouth, cocks in her ass. It was a total cockfest!

The goblins held her arms and legs, letting her know they had full control of her body. She loved it. She loved being their fuck toy, their anal whore, their goblin cum guzzler.

She didn't know if it was some special bonding trait of goblins, but they all came at the same time. She thought getting multiple streams shot into her before was a lot. But it was nothing compared to six goblin cum blasts filling her ass, pussy, and throat all at the same time.

She squealed and thrashed within their strong grips, never having experienced anything like this.

When they pulled out, all six of them splattered her with their cum, so much that her entire body was covered in it.

They collapsed on top of and next to her, draped across her slutty nude body. And promptly fell asleep.

Red glanced at them, listening to their goblin snores. She couldn't move with all of them laying on her, so she decided to lick the cum that was dripping off her lips.

She honestly didn't think she could move anyway, not after a fucking like that. And she supposed snuggling with half a dozen goblins wasn't that bad. They were kind of cute, in their own weird way.

So she nestled her head into the nearest one's chest, content to be covered in goblin bodies and goblin cum.

And glad she had achieved a new feat in her journey to become the ultimate slut in the land!

Chapter 4

Red woke to a disgusting belch. The stench nearly made her wretch. At first, she thought it was one of the naked goblins draped across her cum-stained body. But then she realized it was the tusked toad. And it was rousing itself from its slumber.

"Wake up!" she yelled to the goblins, trying to dislodge herself from the six cocks caressing her body. Normally, she would have been happy to have that many cocks all over her, but one tussle with a horny toad was enough for one day.

"Wat de matter?" the head goblin asked, his dick immediately growing fully erect upon seeing Red's naked tits.

"The toad's waking up!"

"Ahhhhhh!" the six goblins shrieked before leaping to their feet and running around in circles.

Red sighed. Goblins were so weird.

She collected her underwear, cloak, and sword and pointed into the woods. "This way!"

The goblins followed her into the brush just as the toad yawned and smacked its ugly lips, barely escaping its notice. Red was determined to put plenty of distance between the toad and them just in case it caught their scent. That was unlikely, though, since tusked toads had a poor sense of smell.

The goblins eagerly followed her, commenting on how wonderful her ass looked jiggling around as she ran. It probably looked even nicer to them with all their goblin cum on it. And in it. Red was still leaking their goblin gift out of her pussy and ass.

She finally stopped once they were a good distance away from the toad, catching her breath in a lovely copse, the sunlight streaming between the thick branches.

"Yer amazing!" the goblin leader told her.

"Ye save our lives twice!" another said.

"Ye our favorite human ever!" a third effused.

Red blushed. She didn't expect such nice compliments from the goblins, other than on her tits and ass. "Oh, thank you! I love goblin compliments!"

"And we love human females!" a goblin gushed.

"Especially ones that let us fuck der tight asses!" one of his mates added.

The leader raised his non-existent eyebrows. "Want te go one mer round before we part ways?"

Red gazed across their erect cocks and down her cum-covered body. "Sure, why not?"

She rode them in all different positions, making sure each of them got to fill at least one of her holes with their sticky goblin cum.

She collapsed onto her back when they were done, covered in even more cum and feeling like an even bigger slut.

The goblins knelt next to her, holding their cocks.

The leader handed her an intricately carved wooden

whistle. Goblins were known for their woodcarving skills, and the instrument in Red's hands showcased their talent.

"If ye ever in trouble, blow dis and we come running," he told her.

"Oh, thank you, I thought you just wanted me to blow you," she joked.

"Yah, we love the way ye blow. But we also love way ye save us. Ye only human we ever give whistle to."

Red smiled and clutched the wooden instrument to her. "I'm honored. Thank you."

"Ye can also blow it when you want good butt fucking," another goblin said.

"Yah, it real good for dat too," the leader agreed.

Red giggled. Oh, goblins. Though she very well might use it to summon them for a nice six-way ass blasting.

The head goblin moved his cock closer to Red's lips. "Now we do goblin ritual to show we accept ye as part of our tribe."

"What's the ritual?" Red asked. She didn't realize she was becoming part of their collective, but she was moved they held her in such high regard.

"Ye kiss the tip of each of our cocks," the leader replied.

Red smiled. Of course, that's what a goblin ritual entailed. "Okay, let's do it, boys!"

They lined up on their knees, three on each side, and took turns presenting their bulbous heads to her. She kissed each one sweetly, tasting the post-cum that dribbled from their heads.

"How was that?" she asked after smooching every penis.

"Great!" the head gobby replied. "Ye real gud cock kisser."

"Thanks!" Red loved getting compliments on her oral skills.

"We see ye real soon for more gud fucking," he told her before tromping off with his troop.

"Bye bye, beautiful human," they called back before launching into a discordant goblin song.

Red smiled. These goblins might be strange, but they were also sweet. She was developing a fondness for the horny bunch.

She remained on her back, taking some time to recover from all the intense fucking. The sunlight burst through the trees in shafts, making the cum on her sparkle in slutty shininess. Goddess, she was so covered in it. Those goblins had done an amazing job coating her from head to toe.

She finally got to her feet and found a nearby stream, where she cleaned herself as much as she could, though she really needed soap to do a thorough job.

So when she reached Avinnois, she knocked on the first door she came to and asked if she could bathe. Fortunately, a brunette lass answered and was happy to exchange sex for use of her tub. The sex offering was Red's idea. The girl probably would have let her use it for free, but Red believed in always giving something back to those who were kind to her, and sex was the usually the best thing she could give.

So they had fun in the girl's bed, then in the girl's kitchen, and finally in the girl's tub. Girls in Avinnois were known to be particularly beautiful and amorous, and this lass was no exception.

She made a colorful string necklace for Red. The crimson-clad monster hunter attached the whistle to it and hung it around her neck.

The girl gave Red directions to the castle but warned her it was dangerous. Every woman who had journeyed there came back a huge slut.

Red told her she was already a huge slut, so there was nothing to worry about.

She bid the girl adieu with a sweet kiss and a sweeter pat on the butt. And, of course, let the lass take big handfuls of her juicy bottom.

Then she began the hike up the mountain to the forbidding castle. All Red's monster hunting and monster fucking kept her in excellent shape. So she was able to make good time to the peak, where the castle stood on a precipice. It was beautiful in an old world, spooky kind of way: its multiple spires soared heavenward, disappearing among the fluffy clouds.

Red approached the two massive wooden doors, over three times her height. They were adorned with stone knockers in the shape of gargoyle heads. She gripped one of them and knocked.

There was no movement inside. She knocked louder. Still, nothing.

She pushed on the door. To her surprise, it opened. She put her shoulder into it and was able to squeeze through.

It was dark inside, ominous shapes turning into scary

beasts in Red's mind.

She took a step forward. Candles burst into life, illuminating the cavernous foyer. It was grand and elegant, with a large spiraling staircase in the center.

She eyed the flickering flames, realizing there must be magic in the castle, the candles illuminating upon sensing her presence. Red loved magic. Especially when it made her have magically epic orgasms, like Celestine did with her wicked wand. She was looking forward to letting the sexy with and horny horseman dominate her as soon as she returned from her mission.

Something flitted across her vision. A gust whipped her hair across her face and almost extinguished the candles. She spun around but couldn't find any living creature. Perhaps it was just the wind from outside. Or perhaps it was a castle resident.

Red pushed back her hood and placed her hand on the hilt of her sword. The candlelight gleamed off her creamy breasts and thighs. She hoped it would make the master of the castle want to ravish her rather than attack her. She wore skimpy attire in order to defuse hostile situations. And because it made her feel really slutty!

"Hello, anyone here?" she called out. "I'm a girl just out of maidenhood who's a big slut and loves being treated like a sex toy!" She remembered Celestine's warnings about the type of women the master of the castle supposedly enjoyed. So she figured she'd announce her sluttiness right away.

Unfortunately, she got no response to her whorish odes.

"Aw, c'mon, can you please come out? You may have seen some sluts in your day, but I promise I'm the biggest one you'll ever find."

Still no response.

Red pouted. How could the owner of the castle not be enticed by her sexy confessions?

She ticked off a list on her fingers. "I'm a mouth slut, a pussy slut, and, most importantly, a huge ass slut!"

She sensed movement again. Yes! The ass slut bit always got them.

A shadow flitted up the stairs.

"Wait!" Red yelled. "Don't you want my tight little ass?" She barreled up the staircase, determined to confront the creature. It had become a matter of pride now. No one had ever turned down an opportunity to fuck Red in her cute butt. The goblins certainly loved doing it. Which was one reason she liked them so much.

Candelabras came alive when she reached the landing of the second floor. Another glimpse of a shadow ascending even higher.

She went up and up after her quarry, until she reached the top of the highest spire.

There, in the room, was the rose. It floated within a glass case, the just risen moon bathing it in soft light.

Red gasped. She had found the magic item that could cure Harry.

She was so excited her hand slipped off the hilt of her sword as she stepped forward.

And that's when she lost consciousness.

***

She came to lying on a thin mat on the floor. Her cloak was carefully draped over her like a blanket. That made her feel comfy. What didn't make her feel as comfy were the iron bars enclosing her in the small cell she found herself in.

She was a prisoner.

And her warden stepped into view.

She gazed upward at the massive creature before her. He was some type of humanoid beast, covered in brown fur, with a stout nose, sharp teeth, and curved horns on his head.

But what most drew her attention was the beast that was growing between his legs. It was the hugest cock she had ever seen.

It grew and grew, until it passed between the iron bars and bobbed voraciously.

Red gasped. She had never been so happy to be a prisoner.

And was ready for some beastly fun!

Chapter 5

Red couldn't take her eyes off the throbbing cock a few feet away. It was so big Red didn't know if it would fit inside her. But her mind was racing with kinky scenarios of her trying her hardest to shove it in her tight holes.

Her gaze flicked up to the blue eyes of her captor, eyes that looked human and belied the creature's beastly visage.

"Um, hello, I'm Red. Nice, uh, prison cell you have here." She pushed herself up so her cloak fell off, revealing her sexy breasts under her skimpy top.

The creature continued to stare at her, its cock twitching more powerfully.

Red flung her hair over her shoulder. "Hey, don't you know it's polite to introduce yourself when you're shaking a huge penis at a girl?"

"Oh," her captor said in surprise. "Is that now appropriate human etiquette?"

"Sure. It's always nice to know the name of who you're fucking."

"You may call me Beast."

"Is that really your name?"

"It is the only name I go by now."

"Okay, Beast it is!" Red glanced around the dank cell.

"How come you locked me in here?"

"You came here to vanquish me." He nodded at her sword, which lay on the stone floor outside the cell.

"No, no, I promise I didn't."

"You reached for your blade after entering uninvited."

"That's just because your castle is really spooky, and I didn't know what I would find. And I did knock on your ridiculously heavy doors."

"Do you normally enter people's homes if they do not answer?"

"Um, actually, yes. It's usually a good way to ask them if they want to fuck."

The Beast's eyes widened and his cock jumped. "You are a most unusual woman."

"Yup. Now, can you let me out of here?"

"No."

"Aw, c'mon, I told you I'm not trying to hurt you."

"Many who have come to my castle have claimed that. And many have lied."

Red jumped to her feet and put her hands on her hips. "But I'm not lying! I always tell the truth. For example, you have the hugest cock I've ever seen. It's amazing!"

That got the Beast's man, er beasthood, really twitching. He wore no clothes, so there was nothing obscuring his monstrous cock.

"Oh, well, um, thank you."

Red tousled her hair and posed seductively, knowing she had the Beast's attention.

"Come closer," he ordered.

Red smiled and sashayed up to the bars. Yes! She was totally getting some Beast cock.

The furry creature looked her up and down. And then slashed his claws through her clothing. He was so precise he cut the fabric without touching Red's skin.

Her bra and panties fell off, leaving her standing before him completely nude.

"Hey!" Red complained. She didn't mind being naked, but she really liked the underwear Emlyn had given her.

"Prisoners should always be nude," he informed her matter-of-factly.

Red crossed her arms, pushing up her impressive bosom. "What kind of a silly rule is that?"

"A very good silly rule." With that he and his huge cock stomped off.

"Wait! Don't just leave me here! Can't I at least suck that beast cock of yours?"

He didn't answer, the sounds of him clomping down the stairs getting fainter and fainter.

Red plopped onto the mattress and pouted. Stupid Beast. He left her naked and didn't even have the courtesy to give her a proper fucking. Now she would be fantasizing about his dick all night.

Her nipples hardened, which could have been from the slight chill in the tower, but was more likely from her illicit thoughts.

She needed to warm up. She could put her cloak on, but

she had a much better way to generate heat.

She scooted up to the bars imprisoning her and pressed her boobs between them and her pussy against them. Her lower lips eagerly grabbed onto one of the vertical bars, instantly getting wet.

She held onto two other bars and worked her slit up and down the cool iron.

"Ohhhhh yes!!" It felt so good. The fact that she was a prisoner was making her even hornier. "Oh yes, Beast, I'll fuck myself on the bars like a good prison slut!"

Red worked her cunt harder, imagining the Beast had ordered her to fuck herself in the cell. Told her she had to prove to him what a huge slut she was if she wanted any hope of gaining her freedom. Ooh, maybe that is why he imprisoned her. To see just how kinky she could be. Red would show him. She'd be a bigger whore than any slut he had locked up before. Then she'd ride his Beast cock until he filled her with all of his monstrous seed.

Her moans increased as her juices dripped down the bar. "Ohhhh goddess, it feels so good, Beast! I can't stop fucking myself! I love being your slutty prisoner!"

Her screams echoed through the castle. There was no way he couldn't hear her. She hoped he was stroking his Beast cock and imagining her wet and naked.

Red's nipples got harder as her boobs banged back and forth between the bars. Her clit popped out of its hood, which made it easy for her to ram it against the iron and send orgasmic quakes through her body.

"Ohhhhhh fuck, I'm cumming! I'm cumming for you, Beast!" Her juices squirted out of her, splattering the bars and making an impressive puddle just beyond them.

"Ohhhhhhhhhhhhhhhh!" Red screamed, partly for the Beast's benefit, but mostly because she was having one hell of an orgasm. Who knew being a nude prisoner would turn her on so much? Maybe she should ask Celestine to make a magic cell for her where the witch and Harry could watch her fuck herself.

She came a bunch more and finally sank to her knees, panting and clinging to the bars.

"Ohhh goddess, that was good," she whimpered to no one in particular, though perhaps the Beast had a magical listening device and could hear everything she said. That just made her want to be even kinkier!

The Beast tromped back up the stairs. Well, she assumed it was him. She didn't know who else would make such a racket or if anyone else even resided in the castle.

"You are making far too much noise," he bellowed when he stopped in front of the cell.

Red gazed up at him, kneeling in a pool of her own juices. His penis was hidden beneath his massive fur, but flecks of sticky whiteness covered his groin. Aha! He had totally jerked off while listening to her fuck herself. Red would have been upset if all her moaning hadn't turned him on.

"You locked me in this cell. What else am I supposed to do besides squirt all over the place?"

He glanced down and realized he was standing in her

juicy puddle. "You've made a complete mess."

"But a sexy mess!" She remained on her knees, hoping she could coax out his little beast and take it in her mouth.

"How am I supposed to concentrate with you constantly moaning?"

Red huffed. The whole idea was for him to only concentrate on her erotic noises. Geez, what a weird beast. "Concentrate on what? Stomping around the castle."

He stepped closer to the bars, towering over her, and frowned. Apparently, he wasn't used to his prisoners talking back to him.

She smiled up at him. "Listen, why don't you let me out of here and show me around the castle? Then I won't have to make all those sexy noises all the time."

"Y… you want a tour of the castle?"

"Yup."

"With me?"

"Of course. There aren't any other sexy beasts here."

He stroked his furry chin. "You are not what I expected."

"Yup, I'm unique!"

"Do you promise to not make any escape attempts?"

Red held her hand over her heart. "I promise."

The Beast sighed. "Very well." He unlocked the cell with a rusted iron key and swung open the creaky door.

He held his hand out to Red.

"Oh, what a gentleman." She took it and hopped over her cum puddle.

She started down the stairs. "I'll go first, so you can stare at my ass."

That flummoxed the Beast so much he had no response.

"Don't worry, I won't run away. I always keep my promises." She shook her hips back and forth as she descended the stone steps, making sure the Beast got to enjoy every morsel of her sensual booty.

He guided her to a cozy sitting room with ornate furniture and a fireplace with burning embers.

"This is cute," she remarked, spinning around and taking in the room.

"Er, thank you," The Beast replied. "Do you wish to put something on?"

Red glanced down. She was still nude, having left her cloak and torn panties back in the cell. "Nope. I like being naked. But, um, it is a little chilly in here." She rubbed her shoulders, trying to warm up.

"I will stoke the fire." The Beast knelt in front of the mantle and added kindling to the embers, prodding it with an iron poker.

It flamed up nicely, and Red rushed over to it.

"Ohh, that feels nice." She warmed her hands by it, then turned around and wiggled her butt. "I love having a toasty ass!"

The Beast surveyed her curiously. "You are a very strange woman."

"Hey! That's no way to describe your guest."

"You are my prisoner, not my guest."

"Guest, prisoner, what's the difference?"

"Quite a lot."

"Yeah, yeah. Now show me the rest of the castle!" She yanked him towards the door.

"Exactly who is leading this tour?" he grumbled.

"You are. I'm just helping. C'mon!"

The next room he showed her was a massive library. Red had never seen so many books in one place before.

She clutched his arm. His fur was soft and smooth. It felt wonderful beneath her fingers. "Oh my goddess! You have so many books!"

"Yes. This is my favorite room in the castle."

"I can see why." She scampered all over, perusing the spines of as many books as she could. "Yes! You have my favorite." She pulled out a black-bound book and blew off the dust. "The Dragon Princess."

"I have not read that one."

"What?!! It's only the most amazing book ever written!"

She shoved him into a chair with a high back and hopped on his lap. His fur was nice and warm, and Red felt very cozy snuggling up to him.

"What are you doing?" he asked in alarm.

"I'm going to read the book to you. You can't go through life without being exposed to The Dragon Princess."

"I am perfectly capable of reading to myself."

"Yeah, yeah, but it's way more fun if I read to you. Plus, you get to have a cute, naked girl on your lap."

To prove Red's point, the Beast's penis came to life, bumping against her thigh.

She smiled. "See? Isn't that nice?" She placed the book on an end table and straddled the Beast. "We can read after we have some fun."

The Beast's eyes widened. "What kind of fun do you mean?"

She pointed down at his growing cock. "The kind where you stick that beast in my pussy."

"What… but…" he sputtered.

"Aw c'mon, don't you think I'm cute?"

"Y… you are a very beautiful woman."

"Thanks! My pussy's really cute too. I know you're huge, but I really want to see if I can fit you inside me."

His penis was now at its full girth, quivering in anticipation. "I… I would like to try that as well."

"Great!" Red lined up her pussy with his huge, dark brown head. Her body trembled, wondering what it would feel like to take something so big.

She lowered herself onto him.

It was time to tame this Beast!

Chapter 6

Red's entire body trembled as the tip of the Beast's cock touched her lips. She had never had something this huge inside her, and her pussy was quivering in both apprehension and anticipation.

"Oh goddess!"

"What is wrong?" the Beast asked in alarm.

"You cock is so huge. I... I don't know if it'll fit."

"Then perhaps we should not-"

She put a finger to his large lips. "No way. We're doing this! I'll fit it inside me no matter what!"

"You are a very determined woman."

"Yup. Especially when it comes to sex."

"I see. Perhaps it is fortuitous you journeyed here."

"What do you mean?"

"Never mind. You may begin your descent on my penis."

Red rolled her eyes. "Beast! That's not how you talk to someone you're about to fuck."

"It's not?"

"No. You're supposed to say sexy stuff that gets me wet."

"You seemed to have no problem getting wet in your cell. I still expect you to clean up your mess."

"Ooh, like be your sexy nude maid, bending over to lick

up my cum just as you arrive to check on me? You see my ass sticking up and can't resist ramming me with your huge beast-hood!"

"I, uh, was imagining you would use a mop, but that scenario sounds much more intriguing."

Red put her hands on his broad shoulders, straddling him more comfortably. "A mop, huh? What do you want me to do with it?"

"Er, wipe up liquid?"

She sighed and whacked him playfully in the chest. "Beast! That's a normal thing you do with a mop. What kind of sexy thing can you do with it?"

His eyes traveled down Red's curves until they alighted on her pussy, which hovered over his twitching cock. "You wish me to ram the mop handle up your vagina?!"

Red clasped her hands together. "Now you're getting it!"

"I never considered using the instrument in that way."

"You gotta start thinking super-kinky like me."

"I will consider it. But I still want you to clean the castle."

"What?!" Red protested. "You imprisoned me to do your cleaning?" She lowered her hips during her objection, forgetting there was a hardened Beast sword underneath her. She felt her first penetration and immediately rose back up. "Holy shit!!!" She clung to the Beast, her body trembling from just that brief foray into her folds.

"Why did you lower yourself so quickly?" the Beast asked.

"I… I didn't mean to. It's all your fault!"

"My fault?" he grumbled. "You are the one who climbed

on me and have been talking about sex."

"Well, that…" She crossed her arms and pouted. She hated it when sexy Beasts were right. "Okay, that's totally accurate. Let me rub myself along your tip to get nice and wet and get used to your girth."

"Very well."

She snatched the fur on his chest, using it as leverage as she rocked her hips back and forth, moving his bulbous head along her wettening lips. "Oooo yeah. That's nice."

The Beast growled and seized Red's hips, moving her faster over his now-pulsating cock. "Your lips are very succulent."

Red beamed. "I love being told I have succulent lips! So does that mean I don't have to clean your castle?"

"Of course you do. You broke into my domicile. You are lucky I let you out of your cell."

Red stuck her tongue out at him. "Why do you have be such a big meanie?"

"I am not a meanie," he replied, gyrating her faster and getting her incredibly wet. "I am a practical Beast."

"Oh goddess, I'm getting soaked!" Red felt very ready to take her beastly impaling. "How about we fuck and talk about maid duties later?"

The Beast's hands closed tighter around Red's waist. He was so strong she knew he could do whatever he wanted to her. She hoped what he wanted was to force her to take his gigantic cock again and again until he shot all his Beast seed into her.

"I accept," he replied. "I can no longer stand your sexual teasing."

"Teasing? You're the one moving my pussy around your tip and getting me all hot and bothered."

"You're the one who began the teasing. I merely furthered it."

"Ahh, you're so annoying! I need you to fuck me right now!" There was something about the Beast constantly challenging her that was turning Red on. She was pretty sure he secretly liked her but was too grumpy to admit it. So, she'd give him the fucking of his life and turn him into one happy Beast. That is, if she could take his monster of a cock.

He lowered her tiny pussy onto his huge head. He parted her lips, just a sliver of his beast-hood slipping in.

She seized his fur as her entire body tightened. "Ohhhhh fuck!"

"Are you all right?" he asked with concern.

"Y… yes, I… I just can't believe how big you are."

"Do you wish me to continue?"

"Goddess, yes! C… can you just go slow?"

"Of course. I always fuck my maids slowly at first."

"Uhhhhhhhh!" Red moaned as he slid his head inside her. "Y… you're so funny." She didn't expect the Beast to be a comedian, but if his jokes were about her being slutty, she was fully onboard.

She couldn't stop her body from trembling as he lowered her inch by inch. Every inch she thought she wouldn't be able to take any more of his girthy shaft, that her pussy couldn't possibly fit his full sword. But somehow she did. She clung to him tightly, moaning and groaning until she sank to the very bottom of his cock.

A breathless gasp escaped her lips. She could barely form words, barely think. Her entire world became the monstrous cock taking up every inch of her pussy.

"You're trembling," the Beast informed her.

"Uh... uh huh. I... I've never been filled like this before. C... can we just stay like this for a bit so I can adjust to your big beast?"

"Of course. I am impressed you were able to take the whole thing."

"Y... yup. Told you I was a huge slut." She placed her arms against his chest and rested her head against his furriness. He felt both soft and strong. Red could easily envision herself falling asleep on top of him. With his huge cock inside her of course.

He wrapped his paws around her and held her protectively. Red sighed. This was the life. Being held by a furry beast while impaled by his big monster.

"You're very cozy," she told him.

"Thank you," he replied. "Your body also emanates a pleasant warmth."

"Oooh, you little Beast flatterer." His cock throbbed inside her, making Red wiggle on his lap. His big beast was going to take some getting used to.

"Do not get accustomed to it. You are still a trespasser."

"Oh c'mon, can't we just forget that? Especially when I

have your huge cock in my pussy?"

"Do you use sex to get out of all your predicaments?"

"Pretty much."

"Has that been effective?"

"Oh yeah."

"Hmm, your womanhood is gripping me extremely tightly. You will likely make an excellent sex toy."

Red gasped. "You want me to be your sex toy?"

"Er, yes. Did you not want me to speak dirty to you like that?"

"Fuck yeah! I love being a sex toy! I'm very good at it." She squirmed around on his dick and bounced her boobs for him.

"I can see that. Having a sex toy maid does sound appealing."

She rolled her eyes. "You are really into me being your maid. Ohh! I get it. You want me to dress as a sexy maid so you can ravish me in every room in your castle. That will be a good way to do the rest of the tour you promised."

"I did not say I wanted you to dress as a sexy maid."

She rubbed his furry chest. "I bet you have some skimpy maid outfits here."

"Certainly not."

She squeezed his dick with her pussy, and he let out a beastly groan.

"Er, maybe one or two," he panted.

Red smiled. "I knew it! I'll totally try them on as long as you promise to fuck me in every single room."

"We have not even properly made love once. How do you

know you want to do it so many times?"

Red squeezed him again, making both of them moan. "Ohhh, trust me, I know."

She lay against his chest, fantasizing about him tearing off her maid costume and taking her whenever he wanted: up against the bookcase, in front of the fireplace, bent over holding the prison cell bars and begging to be his sex slave for eternity.

"And you are not disturbed by my appearance?" he asked.

Red saw the brief vulnerability in his eyes and wondered if he had locked himself in his castle because he was afraid others would not accept him.

She stroked his cheek. "Not at all. I think you're very handsome, strong, and make an amazing cuddle buddy." She rose up and kissed him. His eyes widened in surprise, but then he kissed her back. His lips were softer than she expected, and she enjoyed the sweet smooch with him.

When she lowered back down, his cock was thrust fully into her again. "Ohhhhhh fuuucckkk!!" She hadn't meant to begin riding him so soon. She wanted a little more time to adjust to his girth. But that first thrust sent so many wonderful vibrations through her, her pussy was screaming at her to continue.

So she grabbed his fur and rose up again. "Ram me up and down on your cock like a fuck toy!" she pleaded.

He snatched her hips and forced her down to his hilt. Red almost blacked out. He was so forceful, and his cock was so huge, Red could barely take the overpowering sensations.

"Ahhhhhh!" the Beast growled. "You are extraordinarily tight!"

"Ohh fuck, thank you! Your cock is dominating my pussy!"

He thrust her up and down again. "You enjoy being dominated, don't you?"

"Ohhhhhhh!" Red shrieked. Every thrust was painful pleasure, one further step in becoming the Beast's whore. "I love it! Please pound me with your huge beast and turn me into your whore! I'll clean your castle and do whatever you want if you treat me like a slut!"

"I have never had a woman so eager to be fucked. I cannot contain myself any longer." The Beast enveloped Red's waist with his huge claws and bounced her on his lap, ramming his cock fully into her every time.

Red let out a staccato of submissive moans, completely giving her pussy over to the Beast. He was so strong and so huge, it took no effort to become his fuck toy.

Red's juices seeped out of her as the monstrous cock plunged into her again and again. Each thrust sent her further into sexual oblivion, where she could think of nothing but being fucked. Fucked again and again until she was begging him to shoot his beastly load inside her.

The Beast's growls got more powerful the more he pounded Red. His cock throbbed insanely hard, like it was on the burst of erupting at any moment.

"I want to see your breasts bounce harder!" he commanded. He went even faster. Red's boobs bounced rapidly under his animalistic gaze. He watched them eagerly, smashing her more powerfully the more they jiggled. Red had never been prouder of her massive tits.

His hands moved from her waist to her ass. They were so big they enveloped both her juicy cheeks. He squeezed her butt powerfully, like it was his property. From the way he was fucking her, she was ready to turn over ownership of her ass and every other naughty part of her.

And she made sure to let him know that.

"Ohhh goddess, Beast! My pussy is yours! My ass is yours! My entire body belongs to you! Please make me cum and shoot your sticky seed into me!"

That sent him into a fucking frenzy. He smashed her up and down at unnatural speeds. Her body flopped around like a rag doll. He had complete control over it and was going to ram her pussy until he had emptied every last drop from his beastly balls.

He found her clit. His hands were so large he could have his fingers on her ass while his thumbs rubbed her inflamed nub.

"Ohhhhh fuck!!" she shrieked. "I... I'm going to cum!"

"So am I!" he growled. His animal noises of pleasure just added to Red's climax.

She shuddered as her orgasm ripped out of her and down the Beast's huge shaft. At the same time, he erupted up into her. She squealed from the tremendous amount of liquid flowing from his loins. She had never been with a creature who could cum so powerfully.

She clung to him and moaned as her juices flowed down and his up. She let him fill her pussy, feeling like a dam about to overflow with his sticky semen.

When he finally lifted her off his cock, his cum poured out of her onto the floor, along with plenty of her own juices. They made a large puddle beneath her, which she would probably have to clean up in a sexy maid costume later. She didn't care. She had just experienced possibly the most intense sex of her life. All she could think about was how she wanted the Beast to fill her with his cock every day.

He placed her back on his lap. She trembled against him, spilling more of her womanhood.

"P… please hold me," she said.

He wrapped his powerful arms around her. She felt warm and cozy and happily eked out the rest of her pussy juices.

"Th… that was wonderful," she sighed, snuggling into his soft fur.

"It was most enjoyable," he agreed. "I believe you are the woman who can help me solve my dilemma."

She stroked his hair. "What's your dilemma?"

"I need a woman to make love to for two days straight, uninterrupted."

"You mean forty-eight hours of non-stop sex?"

"Correct."

Red shivered. Two days of having his ridiculously huge cock inside her, flooding her with his thick cum.

Ohhhhh fuck.

Chapter 7

Red sat naked on the Beast's lap, contemplating the sexy and surprising news from her new lover.

"Why do you need to fuck me for two days straight?" she asked, once again trembling at the thought of his huge beast being inside her for that long.

"I was cursed by a witch," her furry companion replied.

Red threw up her hands. "What's with all these kooky witches and their curses?"

"Pardon."

"Oh, um, I know another guy with a juicy cock who got cursed by a sexy witch."

"Exactly how many juicy cocks have you been taking?"

She ruffled his fur. "Oo, someone's jealous!"

"I certainly am not."

"You want this tight pussy all to yourself, don't you?" She moved his paw between her legs, coaxing him to rub her slit.

"I, er, well it is extremely tight and enjoyable."

"Thanks!" Red loved compliments on her pussy. The Beast rubbed her gently, and she nuzzled against his chest, purring contentedly. "So tell me more about this curse."

"One night, a storm raged outside the castle. An old hag appeared at my door, begging for food and shelter. She offered me an enchanted rose as payment."

Red gazed into his eyes, entranced by the story, and by what he was doing between her legs.

"I spurned her," the Beast continued. "For she was ugly and repulsive."

"That wasn't very nice," Red commented.

"I am aware," he growled. "May I finish my tale?"

"Sure, Mr. Grumpy Pants. Just keep massaging my pussy!"

He frowned at her impudence but continued tickling her lovely lips. "The hag transformed before my eyes into a beautiful enchantress and scolded me for only seeing what was on the surface. As punishment, she turned me into a beast, cursed to remain as such unless I could find a partner to make love to for two days straight."

Red opened her legs, allowing him better access. He was very good at pussy rubbing. "That's a weird requirement. But a sexy one! I bet she was one horny enchantress!"

"Perhaps. All I know is she left the rose and said if I could complete the task, the rose would be bestowed with the power to lift any curse."

"That's great!" Red exclaimed.

"It is?"

"Sure. All I have to do is let you ram my pussy for forty-eight hours. Easy."

"Easy?" He stopped playing with her pussy, staring at her incredulously.

"Well, maybe not easy. But I'm up for the challenge! I can't claim to be the biggest slut in the land if I don't try sexy stuff like this."

"You… are a most curious woman."

"And a most beautiful woman?"

"Yes."

"A most sexy woman?"

"Very."

"A most wonderfully fantastic woman who never has to clean castles?"

"Don't push your luck."

Red sighed. Well, it was worth a shot.

She rubbed his furry cheeks. "So that's why you got so mad when I got near the rose."

"Yes. I thought you were trying to steal it, thus eliminating any chance I had to break the curse."

"I wasn't trying to steal it. I just wanted to borrow it to help a friend with his own curse."

"Are you a professional curse breaker?"

Red giggled. "Nope. I'm a professional slut."

The Beast nodded approvingly. "I believe I've found the right woman for the job."

"You sure did. Oh, I'm also a professional monster hunter."

"But you are not trying to hunt me."

She kissed him on the cheek. "Of course not. You're not a monster. You're a sexy Beast."

"I am?"

"Yup. With a huge, sexy cock." She tapped the bulbous head of his not-so-little beast, and it sprang to life. "But if you want to fuck me, you gotta catch me!" She hopped off his lap and bolted out of the library.

"Get back here, you naked scamp!" he called, running after her.

Red wound up getting her tour, just not in the way she initially expected, as the Beast pursued her through virtually every room in the castle.

Finally having enough of her shenanigans, he dropped to all fours, greatly increasing his speed.

He easily caught up to her, pouncing on her naked body and pinning her to the carpet.

She smiled up at him, feeling his hot breath on her face. "So, what room is this?"

"The guest bedroom."

Red tilted her head back, getting an inverted view of the room: an ornate wardrobe, cozy fireplace, and canopy bed were the main features. "Looks like a good place to fuck!"

"Indeed." The Beast forced her legs open and impaled her, his girthy weight bearing down on her.

"Ohhhhh fuck, I'm a Beast slut!" she cried. "Ram me with your huge cock!"

He pounded her incredibly hard. Red was pinned under his body, helpless to his beastly fucking. And she loved it. The less control she had, the more turned on she got. Though she appreciated he wasn't putting his full weight on her. He was so large, he'd likely break some bones if he did. But he let enough of his furriness press down on her to show her he was in charge of her pussy. And he was going to fill it with his beastly seed.

She screamed and moaned, never having been speared so deeply. Goddess, she loved beasts!

He fucked her until he filled her creamy cunt.

Then she was on top of him, cumming some more.

Then she was on her hands and knees with him behind her.

Then she was in his arms up against the wall.

Then she was in every other kinky position she could think of, taking his seed and spilling her own juices.

She finally collapsed on top of him, riding his chest as it rose and fell. "Oh wow, you're a real beast in the bedroom."

"Th… thank you. But you need to work on your witticisms."

"My witticisms are amazing, thank you very much. As is my very sore pussy."

"Indeed. But there is a problem."

"Hey! There's not a problem with my pussy."

"No, it's wonderful. I mean, we were only making love for an hour, two at the most. And we are both exhausted."

Red nodded. "Oh, right. So how are we going to last for two straight days?"

"Exactly."

She lowered her head to his chest. Hmm, maybe this non-stop fuck-a-thon would be harder than she thought.

"Oh, I've got it."

"Got what?" he replied.

"A way for us to fuck all day and night."

"And how will we do that?"

"A rare fruit is supposed to grow in Avinnois: purple pommerac. It's said to make people super-horny and give them crazy sexual endurance."

"I have never heard of this. Are you sure you're not making it up?"

"I never make up stuff that has to do with sex. Besides, I have it on good authority from the pretty lass I fucked in town on the way here."

"Exactly how many people have you had sex with?"

"Um, how much time do you have?"

The Beast's eyes narrowed. "You are an extremely naughty woman."

"Yup!" Red replied proudly.

"Naughty women should be punished."

"We sure should! Throw me over your lap and spank me, you powerful Beast!"

He did just that. He sat on the edge of the bed, Red sprawled across his massive legs, and delivered booty-quaking blasts to Red's supple bottom.

"Oh goddess, you spank hard!" she cried, the blows almost bringing tears to her eyes.

"Is it too much for your naughty rear end?"

"Fuck no! I love it rough!"

Red continued to groan and moan, her pussy getting wetter with every powerful ass slap.

When the Beast was done, Red's ass was burning. It was too sore to sit on, so she remained on his lap, grinding her hips against his thigh until she came spectacularly across his legs.

"Ohhhh fuck, that feels better!" she panted after she was done squirting.

"I'm glad to hear it. But you've made another mess."

"Hey, this one is totally your fault. Your spankings made me super-horny."

"You are always horny."

"That's why I'm the right girl to help you break the curse," Red replied cheerfully.

That got a smile out of the Beast. He gently rubbed her back, giving her time to recover from his Beast booty blasts.

"The sun is about to set," he told her. "We should get some rest and set out for your horny fruit at first light."

"Aha! So you do believe me."

"Well, it will not hurt to see if your information is correct."

"Right!" Red hopped off his lap, her butt feeling better. "Let's go to bed."

"You may sleep in this room," the Beast said.

"Where's your room?" Red asked.

"Right across the hall."

"Great! I'll sleep there."

He leapt to his feet. "What?! You want to kick me out of my own room?"

"No, silly. I want to sleep with you in your room."

The Beast's face softened. "You do?"

"Of course. C'mon." She grabbed his paw and yanked him out one set of doors and through another. It was a similar set-up but with an even larger bed, fit for a Beast. "Oh yeah, this bed looks more comfy."

She jumped onto the mattress, sinking into its cushiness and rubbing her naked limbs along the sheets.

The Beast watched her. "You are going to sleep naked?"

"You're the one who said I couldn't wear clothes."

"Oh. Right. Yes, that, um, was a very good rule I made."

"It sure was. Now, are you going to join me?" She patted the spot next to her.

The Beast clambered in, lying on his back. Red nestled up to him, resting her head against his chest and wrapping her leg around him. He was the softest and furriest partner she had ever slept with.

"Mmm, you make a wonderful pillow," she murmured.

"I… am glad to hear it." The Beast wrapped his arms around her, adding to the comforting warmth.

Red fell asleep almost instantly, feeling safe and content.

And ready to be fucked for two straight days!

Chapter 8

Red woke to a cocoon of coziness. The Beast's fur was so warm and soft she could have stayed snuggled against him all day.

But they had a horny fruit to find. And she had some horny shenanigans of her own to take care of. Everyone knew the best way to start the day was by having sex.

The Beast was still asleep, snoring lightly and looking quite adorable. Though he acted gruff, Red knew her furry lover had a soft side. And what better way to access it than by waking him up with a blowjob.

She carefully slid out of his grasp and down his body, until she came to his little beast. Which wasn't little at all. It was at full mast, sticking straight up and begging for attention. Just like human males, he had a serious case of morning wood: perfect for what Red had planned.

There was only one problem. He was so big she didn't know how she was going to fit him in her mouth. She leaned over him, peering at the beastly cock from all angles, trying to find the best way to approach it. Initiating oral sex was a fine art after all.

Her breath fell hot upon his shaft, making it quiver. Red smiled. She loved the way it bobbed and throbbed. It made her want to suck him even more.

Red moved her lips to his bulbous head. Just before she touched it, the Beast stirred.

He gazed down his massive body at her, perched over his quivering cock. "Good morning."

"Morning!" she replied chipperly.

"What exactly do you think you're doing?"

"Trying to figure out how to suck your cock."

"Oh. Is that normally how you start your day?"

"Yup. Or by eating a juicy pussy."

The Beast's penis throbbed harder. He was obviously envisioning her going down on some sexy girl. Red would happily eat out all the lasses in Avinnois if he wanted to watch. And if it spurred him to give her a huge pussy workout afterwards.

"I do not object to this morning ritual," the Beast said with just the hint of a grin.

"Great! But, um, you're too big."

"You did not seem to be complaining about that last night."

"Nope. I was screaming and moaning in ecstasy last night."

"Indeed. Your noises are quite enjoyable."

"Thanks! I aim to please! Okay, let me try this." She flicked her tongue along the head of his cock. It twitched and throbbed, expanding slightly.

"Ahhhhh," the Beast growled. "Do more of that."

"You got it!" Red circled her tongue around his tip, loving

the reactions she was getting from him: both from how his cock moved and from the guttural groans he made.

After getting him worked up from her tongue magic, she placed her lips on his beasthood. She kissed it softly, tasting his animal mustiness. She peppered him with a few more kisses before wrapping her lips around his huge head.

"By the gods!" The Beast thrashed in the bed, his cock twitching in Red's mouth. That was the reaction she wanted. She sucked on his head while stroking his shaft with both hands.

"Uhhhhh, y… you are very talented," he told her.

"Thank you!" she replied, momentarily taking her lips from his girthy beast before taking more of him in her mouth. He was much too big to deep throat, but Red took as much of his wonderful cock as she could.

The Beast seemed to greatly enjoy it, convulsing on the bed while running his paws through Red's lush hair.

Before long, his cock was pulsing out of control in Red's mouth.

"Ahhhhhhh!" he growled. "I… I'm going to explode!"

He did. Really explode. Right into Red's mouth and down her throat. She hung on for dear life as his hips bucked, determined to swallow every last drop of his beastly seed.

He had a stronger taste than most men, more primal and masculine. It just made Red want him even more.

She sucked him dry. Well, almost dry. She made sure he had enough left in him so when she removed her mouth he splattered her face and tits.

He remained on his back, panting and leaking out the last few drops from his phenomenal penis. "I... I have never had anyone swallow so much of me before."

"Told you I was a huge slut. I love drinking Beast cum!"

"You apparently love wearing it too." He eyed her cum-stained face and breasts.

She grinned. "Uh huh. Does it make you want to do anything?"

"Indeed." He snatched her with his powerful hands and deposited her thighs on either side of his face. And proceeded to have beastly fun with her pussy.

"Oh fuck, what a tongue!" Red cried. The Beast's agile instrument was longer and more textured than any other she had experienced. At his first lick along her lips, she got crazy wet. So wet that he slipped inside her with ease, the layered grooves on his tongue touching all her most sensitive spots.

"Ohhhh fuck, Beast! Th... that feels so good! Please don't stop!"

He curled into her special spot, rubbing it so powerfully she had to grip the headboard to stop herself from bucking off him.

She had never experienced a tongue that filled her so much before. It was so long it reached all the way to her cervix, so thick it seemed to touch every part of her pussy.

"Ohhh goddess, Beast!" she screamed, completely lost in sexual bliss. She could no longer hold on to the bed. She thrashed uncontrollably, the Beast's strong hands the only thing keeping her in place.

He continued to tongue fuck her deep and hard. She continued to moan for him and tell him what a huge slut she was. Until she could no longer contain herself.

"Ahhhhhhh, Beast, I… I'm going to cum!"

An earthquake ripped through her body, shaking her from head to toe as her orgasm exploded out of her. Her hips made non-stop gyrations while her pussy squirted non-stop horny juices.

The Beast eagerly lapped them up, not relenting at all with his attack on her tender insides. She loved that he was just as happy to drink up her cum as she was his. The best partnerships always involved mutual cum-drinking.

When she was mostly done squirting, she flopped onto her side. The Beast took her in his arms and kissed her. His fur tickled her cheeks, but his lips were strong and passionate. She eked out the remainder of her juices while sharing sweet smooches with him.

"Ooh, Beast, you're so romantic," she told him while she played with his fur.

"I am?"

"Yup. I knew you were an old softie under all that grumpy gruffness."

"I am not grumpy or gruff."

"Well, sure, not after fucking me a whole bunch."

"Are you saying your womanhood cures people of grumpiness?"

"Yup!"

He ran his paw over her hip and squeezed her ass. "I

cannot argue with that."

"Good. Then let's get some breakfast before we head out."

Red cooked in the nude for him, shaking her tush as she fried up some eggs from the chickens he kept next to the castle. That got her more than a few spankings. She was happy he couldn't resist touching her cute butt.

When they were done eating, they marched out of the castle, Red clad in only her crimson cloak.

"Do you not wish to wear more than that?"

"Well, some ravenous Beast tore my panties to shreds."

Red thought she detected a hint of a blush on his furry cheeks.

"Yes, er, I might have been a bit too hasty."

"Oh don't worry. I love getting my clothes ripped off. It's hot!"

"I will happily rip apart any clothing you put on."

"Aww, you're so sweet." She took in his equally nude form, a blue cape strung around his neck. "You know you're just as naked as me."

"I am a Beast. I'm covered in fur." That was true. His brown fur concealed him. Except when he got an erection. Then his big beast sprang out for all to see.

"Well, you can use your cozy fur to keep me warm if it gets too cold."

He nodded. "I must admit, you are an enjoyable person to share body heat with."

"Oh yeah, I'm an amazing cuddle buddy."

"If this fruit does what you believe, we will likely be

cuddling for a very long time."

"Fuck yeah! I can't wait."

The Beast's eyes widened. "You are very excited about the non-stop lovemaking."

"Yup." She put her hand in his oversized paw. "I'm looking forward to making love to you for two straight days."

"But you just met me."

"I'm an excellent judge of character. And an even better judge of big cocks!" That got his penis to leap from beneath his fur. "Ha! See, your fur doesn't cover everything. Not when you get horny."

"I would not be getting horny if you stopped talking about my, er…"

"Big beast? Sweaty salami? Pulsating pussy pounder?"

His erection grew, bobbing before her eyes. "Yes, that," he replied, growing more embarrassed.

She ran her fingers through her hair, pushing her cloak aside to make sure he could see all of her curvy nudeness. "Well, maybe you should take care of that erection."

His eyes traveled up and down her body. "If we keep fucking, we will never find the purple pommerac."

"Oh, fine," she pouted. She knew he was right, but she really wanted that juicy cock.

They proceeded into the mountainous terrain near the castle, the area where the pommerac was supposed to grow. Red led the way, making sure to swish her cloak to the side from time to time so the Beast could see her naked butt. It was important to remind him how bouncy it was. And how ripe it was to be squeezed by his powerful paws.

After a couple of hours of searching, they had no luck. They continued their ascent, unwilling to give up.

The air got colder. Red's nipples got harder. She was about to ask the Beast if she could snuggle up against him when a creature leapt in front of them.

It had the lower body of a human male and the upper body of a mountain goat. Red recognized it immediately as a gringat. They were found in mountainous regions and were quite territorial.

Though this one apparently had something else on its mind. Upon seeing Red, its cock grew to a very impressive length.

It brayed, making guttural noises Red knew were gringat mating calls.

Her eyes got big.

This could definitely be a problem.

Chapter 9

The Beast leaped in front of Red, growling at the gringat. Apparently, he didn't appreciate the goat creature's erection as much as Red.

The gringat scuffed its hooves along the ground. While most of its lower body was human, its feet were more like that of a goat.

It snorted at the Beast. Who snorted right back.

Red knew what was coming. "Beast, wait, you don't have to-"

Too late. Her furry companion rushed forward just as the gringat charged.

Red sighed. Why did males always have to prove who had the bigger sword? They should be using those swords to spear her tight little pussy.

The gringat lowered its horns, trying to ram the Beast.

The two large creatures met with a crunch that reverberated through the mountains. The Beast grabbed the gringat's horns, wrestling with it and trying to gain the upper hand.

Red's gaze switched between their massive torsos and the massive cocks swinging between their legs. Talk about a sexy show!

But Red didn't want them to fight. She didn't want the Beast to get hurt. And the gringat wasn't doing anything wrong. It was just acting according to its nature. If anything, it was flattering that the creature immediately wanted to mate upon seeing Red's naked body.

She flung her cloak into the air. The sunlight glistened off the crimson fabric, drawing both the Beast and the gringat's eyes upward.

In that momentary distraction, Red ran up the goatman's back and acrobatically flipped inbetween them.

She put a gentle hand on their furry chests. "Now, boys, we can handle this in a more civilized way, don't you think?"

Their hostilities were forgotten as they gazed upon Red's nudeness.

"This is not a creature to be reasoned with," the Beast complained. He had a point. Since they had the heads of goats, gringats couldn't speak, except in their noisy goat way. But Red had other ways to communicate.

"Oh, I can reason with him." She grabbed the gringat's cock and began stroking it. It brayed and moaned, its erection twitching in Red's hand.

"Red, what do you think you're... uhhhhhh!" The Beast's protest was interrupted by Red snatching his cock as well.

"Now isn't that better?" she asked the two furry creatures trembling on either side of her. They towered over her, and their cocks were massive. Fortunately, she was an expert at giving handjobs, especially to non-human creatures.

The goat stamped its feet some more, but this time in

pleasure, its cock pulsating powerfully between Red's dexterous fingers.

The Beast's cock, which was even larger, was doing similar gymnastics. He growled and grabbed Red's hair, tugging it.

The gringat did the same thing, so she had two strong creatures pulling her long locks.

"Ahh, easy boys. There's enough of me to go around." She pumped them harder, secretly liking that they were manhandling her. Or should it be Beast-handling? Goat-handling? Well, whatever it was, she liked it.

Both male creatures made increasingly loud noises until their cocks throbbed so much they could no longer stand it. They erupted at the same time, spewing so much semen it was like they were competing to see who could cum the most. Red loved competitions like that!

She twirled in a circle between them, letting them cover her in as much of their seed as they wanted.

When they were done, they sank to their knees, panting.

She put her arms around their broad shoulders, her cum-covered tits at the level of their faces. "Now, doesn't that feel better?"

"M… much better," the Beast agreed, shooting out another glop of his beastness.

The gringat did the same, snorting happily.

Red smiled. She loved having satisfied customers.

The goatman was so satisfied he immediately got a full erection again. Red's eyes went wide. Goodness, he was as horny as the Beast.

Her eyes got even bigger when she glanced at her companion. His cock was in mid-growth. She got to watch it expand before her eyes until it reached full mast, quivering anxiously. She licked her lips. Even though he and the gringat were no longer fighting, they were still comparing their swords. Well, that was great news for Red. She loved taking huge cock swords.

"It seems this creature has not been satisfied," the Beast said.

"Nope," Red replied. "Guess I'll just have to fuck him."

"What?!"

"You know, take his big goat cock."

"I know what fucking means."

"Then why you'd act all surprised?"

"You cannot fuck this goat creature."

"Why not?"

"Well, he... that is..." The Beast furrowed his brows, evidently flummoxed to come up with a reason.

"You better not say he's a weird creature. You don't like people saying that about you, right?"

The Beast stared at her. Then his shoulders sagged. "You are correct. I do not."

"You shouldn't. Those people are stupid. You're a sexy Beast!"

That got a smile out of him. "Thank you. However, I, er, that is..." His furry face flushed.

Red scrutinized him. There was obviously something he was embarrassed to say.

She hopped forward, pinning his cock between her thighs, and shimmied back and forth. "Does this make you want to tell me?"

He moaned and clutched her shoulders, thrusting between her legs. Fuck, his big beast felt so good rubbing against her supple thighs.

"I… I want to be the only one to fuck you," he finally admitted.

"Aha! You are jealous."

"No. That is ridicul… uhhhhhh!" Red squeezed his cock tighter. "V… very well, maybe I am a little jealous."

She released his beasthood, leaving him panting. "That's okay. I like that you want me all to yourself."

"Y… you do?"

"Sure. But here's a secret. I become an even bigger slut when I'm getting pounded by two sexy beasts at the same time. So why don't you both fuck me and I'll be so horned up I'll do whatever you want later."

The Beast's large eyes got even larger. "That is a very acceptable compromise."

Red smiled. She thought he would like it.

The gringat hopped around, obviously not understanding any of their conversation. But obviously getting more excited as his cock bobbed rapidly.

Red pointed to her ass, then bent over and spread her cheeks. She hoped this would let the goat creature know where she wanted him to fuck her. She'd let the Beast handle her pussy. He had the biggest cock, and that belonged in her cozy cooch. Not that she wasn't going to let him plunder her ass later. She really wanted to see if she could fit something so large in her tight booty. But the gringat's dick would be a good warm-up.

The goatman seized her hips and pressed his human cock against her tiny opening.

Red jumped and spun around, putting her hands on his chest. "Wait! Let me lubricate my slutty butt first. You're too big to go in right away."

The creature looked at her quizzically but was happy to wait once he saw Red insert two fingers into her pussy.

Both he and the Beast began stroking their cocks.

Red glanced between the two juicy salamis. "You boys like watching me play with myself, huh?"

"Very much," the Beast grunted.

"Brahhhhh!" the gringat brayed. Red was taking that as a "yes."

She worked her cunt over harder, until her fingers were completely coated in her essence.

She removed them and reached around until her index finger found her tiniest opening. She pierced her ass, groaning deliciously as she did.

"Ohhhh fuck! I... I don't usually finger my ass."

Her male companions stroked their girths more vigorously.

"You should do it often," the Beast encouraged.

The gringat moaned its assent.

"Okay!" Red readily agreed. She dove deeper into her tight

ass, getting it nice and lubricated. She realized she should probably play with it more regularly. With all the anal sex she'd been having lately, it was important to keep her ass in tip top fucking shape.

After a bunch of sexy groans and moans, she finally popped out her digit. "Okay, my ass and pussy are ready to be fucked!"

The Beast seized her hips and lifted her off the ground. He was so much taller than her, the only way for them to fuck standing up was if her feet were flailing. Which just made her feel more under his beastly power.

He lowered her onto his shaft. She clung to him, moaning and whimpering at how ridiculously big he was.

She sank to his hilt, squirming and feeling like her pussy belonged to him.

And then her ass was raided. The gringat pressed his huge head against her tiny opening and penetrated her.

"Ohhhhhhh fuuuckkkkkk!" she wailed. That spurred the goatman on. He pushed upward until he got as far into her as possible.

Red convulsed between the hairy bodies, her mind almost overloaded with the dual sensations filling her.

"Are you all right?" the Beast asked.

"Y… yes. I… I just have never had two cocks this big inside me at the same time before. It… it's… ohhhhhhhhh!" She dissolved into moans, putting her head against the Beast's strong chest. Her pussy and ass were throbbing, screaming at her that she was crazy to invite in these two behemoths. But also telling her she should absolutely not remove the delicious cocks. Her pussy and ass could be very contradictory at times.

"Please fuck me," she begged quietly. It was hard for her to process words. Hard to do anything but turn her body over to them as their naked fuck toy.

The Beast and gringat began working in tandem, having forgotten their feud now that they had a luscious human female to fuck.

Red was squeezed between them, helpless to move. Helpless to do anything except take their huge shafts in her way-too-tiny holes.

Both creatures grunted loudly, their cocks throbbing inside Red, acting as if they had never experienced such lovely tightness before.

Red smiled through her moaning. She was happy her tight pussy and ass was so exhilarating for them. Their cocks were certainly exhilarating for her.

They went harder, the sounds of them slapping against her pussy and ass getting louder and louder. Red wondered if their noises would attract other mountain critters, who would come watch a helpless slut get pounded by two huge beasts.

"Ohhhh goddess!!" she shrieked. "Fuck me harder! Make me your pussy slut! Your ass slut! The biggest slut who's ever lived!!" She was completely lost in the nirvana of the dual fucking. Her pussy and ass were burning. Burning with the desire to never be freed of their monstrous captors, namely the Beast and gringat's pulsating cocks.

They smashed her harder than any humans could. They

were lost in their animal need to spew their seed into her.

And before long they did. The Beast and gringat's roars created a strange cacophony, joined by Red's higher-pitched screams of bliss.

She came hard as they pumped their semen into her. And boy did they pump it. Red squealed and squirmed, feeling the thick liquid pour into her ass and pussy.

When she thought they were finally spent, they got a second wind and shot even more into her.

All three of them finally collapsed on the ground, the Beast and gringat's limbs strewn over Red. She tried to catch her breath, their cum freely leaking out of both her holes.

The gringat leaped to his feet, snorted happily, and bounded off. Apparently, Red's butt had satisfied his primal need.

Red turned on her side and cuddled against the Beast. "Oh goddess, I have so much cum in me."

He held her protectively, shivering from the post-coitus. "Was it too hard? It is difficult not to empty myself into such a wonderfully tight womanhood."

Red smiled into his fur. He said the sweetest things. "No, it was wonderful. I think I'm just going to be leaking cum out of me the rest of the day."

"You certainly seemed to satisfy that creature."

Red gazed up at him. "Did I satisfy you?"

The Beast brought her to his lips, kissing her deeply. "It would be impossible to satisfy me any more."

She nestled into him. "You're such a sweet Beast."

"I thought I was gruff and grumpy."

"Well, yeah, but my pussy is making you much sweeter." She giggled, rubbing her lower lips against him.

"You are quite ridiculous." He tickled her sides.

She squirmed within his strong grasp. "Ahh! Stop! You're making me leak out more cum."

"Is that not good? Your vagina should be free to be filled again later."

"Oh right. You're going to be filling it non-stop once we find the pommerac."

"Indeed." The Best grinned. Which made Red grin. Oh yeah, she had totally gotten him to go from grumpy to horny.

They continued up the mountain, Red leaving glops of Beast/gringat cum along the way. Her friends Hansel and Gretel liked leaving breadcrumbs to trace their return route in unfamiliar territory. She preferred leaving a trail of juicy cum.

The air got chillier. Red's nipples got harder. She clasped her cloak around her, wondering if she should ask the Beast to press his cozy body against her.

But then they came upon an impasse: a large rock formation with curious symbols.

Red rushed up to it. "Beast, look! The purple pommerac." A flower had been drawn on the stone, dyed with purple pigment.

The Beast knelt to examine it. "Hmm, I do not see any in the vicinity."

Red traced her fingers along the stone. She felt grooves that ran up and around in an arc. "I think there's a hidden doorway here."

Her companion dug his claws into the grooves. "Stand back."

She gave him room and watched him try to pry open the stone doorway. He grunted. His muscles strained. But the rock didn't move.

He stepped back and let out an exasperated growl.

Red hugged him. "Don't worry. I had fun watching you use your sexy muscles. It got me wet!"

The Beast glanced at her glistening lips. "Perhaps I should keep trying then."

"Or we could figure out another way in. Look over here." She led him around the right side of the formation. There, protruding from the wall was a stone phallus.

"What in the world is that?" the Beast asked.

"A big stone dick," Red replied, like it was a very natural occurrence.

"Why is it here?"

"For me to fuck!"

"Red, you do not have to fuck every phallic object you encounter."

"Blasphemy! Besides, it's obviously a secret lever to open the passageway."

"Why do you think that?"

"Why else would someone put a stone cock here?"

The Beast sighed. "You have your own unique logic."

"Thank you!"

She dropped to her hands and knees.

"Time to fuck a sexy rock!"

Chapter 10

Red backed up on all fours until her pussy touched the rock hard cock. It was literally rock hard as it was a big stone phallus protruding from the hill.

"Ohhhhh," she moaned as it parted her lips. "This mountain knows how to make a girl feel like a slut!"

The Beast peered down at her as she wiggled her way onto the stone shaft. "You are a very unusual girl."

"Hey, this unusual girl lets you fuck her a whole bunch."

The Beast stroked his chin. "Yes. That is most enjoyable."

Red worked her hips all the way back until she had taken the entire stone penis. Fuck, it felt good. But she needed more. "You know what's also enjoyable? You sticking your big beast in my mouth!"

The Beast's huge cock sprang to life. "You want me in your mouth while you fuck the mountain?"

"Yup. Spit-roast me good!"

The Beast fell to his knees, presenting his quivering cock to Red's lips. She instantly took him in her mouth as she rocked her hips back and forth, fucking herself on the stone phallus. She loved being fucked in two holes at once. It made her feel like a helpless slut.

While she still couldn't take all of the beast's huge sword, she got more of it in her throat this time. It was ridiculous how big he was, but it just made her want him more. Want him to spew his musky liquid into her mouth and make her drink it all up.

She smashed her pussy on the rock cock harder while she enjoyed the meaty member in her mouth.

The Beast groaned in pleasure, grabbing her hair with both hands and helping her take more of his beasthood.

Her pussy was dripping all over the stone dick, and her saliva was dripping all over the Beast's dick.

She loved how the mountain's penis was filling her. With this and the vines that had recently fucked her, she was discovering just how fun nature could be.

So much fun that she came all over the mountain, squirting her pussy juice across its face and cock. At the same time, the Beast shot his load down her throat, holding her tightly against him so she had to gulp down every last drop of his beastly seed. She closed her eyes and happily took all that he had to give.

When he was done unloading an inordinate amount of cum, he pulled her off his cock. She gasped and stared up at him like a very happy slut.

"Wow, that was a lot of cum," she remarked.

"Apologies," he replied. "I hope it was not too much for you."

"Heck no. I love gulping down your beastiness."

The Beast smiled and glanced at the puddle between her legs. "It seems you had plenty of fluid loss yourself."

"Oh yeah. I fucked that stone cock good!"

As if in response to her sexual prowess, the doorway they had discovered slid open with a ponderous groan.

Red eased herself off the cock and jumped up. "See? I knew fucking that thing would be the key."

The Beast harrumphed. "I think you just want an excuse to fuck every phallic object you see."

"That too!"

Red rushed to the opening and peered in, cum still dripping from her pussy. The Beast came up behind her, his warm body pressed against her, his cock rubbing against her back.

Red leaned in farther. "It's really dark. I can barely see anything."

The Beast moved with her. "Be careful, there may be a dro… ahhhhhhh!"

"Eeeeeeek!" Red echoed as the ground dropped out beneath them.

They tumbled down a steep slope, the Beast clutching Red to him.

At the end of the not-so-fun slide, he landed on his back. Red bounced off him and came straight down with her legs spread. And got completely speared by his very erect cock. She slid all the way down it and screamed loudly. The force of taking something that huge so suddenly almost made her lose consciousness.

It had a similarly powerful effect on the Beast: he came instantly, shooting straight up into her engorged pussy.

"Ohhhhhh fuuucckkkk!" she shrieked, squirming uncontrollably from the deep penetration and the warm liquid filling her.

"By the gods!!" the Beast growled, seizing Red's hips and pumping round after round of his beastly semen into her.

Red collapsed onto his chest, breathing hard.

The Beast enveloped her in his massive arms. "Are… are you all right?"

"Y… yeah. I… I just wasn't prepared to take your full beast like that."

"I apologize. I did not intend to-"

"Are you kidding?" she said, cutting him off. "It felt great!"

"So you do not wish me to pull out of you?"

"Heck, no." She wiggled around on top of him, finding the perfect place for him to rest inside her pussy.

"But I am still leaking inside you."

"Leak away! My pussy is the perfect place for your Beast cum."

The Beast rubbed her back. "Good. For there is no other place I wish to put it."

Red kissed his chest. "Aww, you're such a sweet little Beast." His big beast continued to expand and contract inside her, leaking out everything it had. There were few places as warm and inviting for beast seed as Red's cute cunt.

They finally got up, Red sliding off the Beast's penis with a mournful gasp. Sunlight streaked through an opening high above them, illuminating several stalagmites clustered together.

Red weaved between them and eyed another stone door on the other side of the chamber. "Looks like we have another sexy puzzle to solve."

"Why do we have to go through these ridiculous games?" the Beast grumbled.

"Because for something as amazing as a fruit that lets you fuck all day and night, we have to earn it."

"Hmm," the Beast replied, not entirely convinced.

"You want to break the curse, don't you?"

"Yes, of course."

"And you want to fuck me a bunch more, right?"

"Oh yes."

"Great. Then stop grumbling and help me figure out the trick to opening this door."

The Beast prowled around, sniffing with his cunning nose. "I do not see any stone phalluses."

Red licked her lips. "I do."

"What? Where?"

Red pointed to the large rocks jutting up from the ground. They had rounded tips, just like the head of a juicy penis.

"You cannot be serious," the Beast said.

"I'm always serious when it comes to my pussy getting plundered."

"Those are much too large. Even for a slut of your stature."

"Thank you!" Red was never offended when she was called a slut. It was a mark of pride for her. "But I won't take the whole thing, just the top of each one where it's skinniest."

The Beast considered this. "I suppose that's possible. Though even the tops of these stone formations are quite large."

"That's why all the practice with your big beast was so helpful."

The Beast's cock twitched. "Er, I… am glad I could be of assistance."

"Ooh, look at that!" Red pointed to the bases of the stalagmites. A glowing circle of light appeared on one, then moved to another, and another. "I bet that's the order I have to fuck them in."

The Beast rolled his eyes. "Is this more of your unique logic?"

"Yup. But, hey, it worked on the cock outside."

The Beast muttered under his breath, knowing he couldn't dispute Red's sexy success. "How will you get from one to the other so quickly? You'll have to climb each one to reach its tip."

She sidled up to him, nudging him with her hip. "That's where you come in. You're easily tall enough, so you can carry me around, slamming my pussy down on each stone shaft in time with the lights."

The Beast was speechless for a moment. "That will entail rapid spearing on many different stone penises. It will likely cause great strain on your lovely vagina."

Red clutched his arm. "Aww, you think it's lovely? Thanks, Beastie!"

Her companion mumbled something about that nickname

not being his favorite. But she ignored him, too excited about the upcoming fucking.

"Anyway, damn right it will be a strain," she continued. "I'm already getting wet thinking about it!"

The Beast's gaze traveled between his companion's legs. Her lips were once again moist. "Very well. But you must inform me if it gets to be too much for you."

"Will do. Now lift me up and treat me like your personal fuck toy!"

The Beast snatched Red around the waist and strode to the nearest stalagmite, waiting for the sequence of lights to reach it.

"Now!" Red cried when the rock's base glowed. And then she cried much louder as the Beast brought her pussy down upon its tip. "Holy rock cocks!! It's so big!!" Her entire body convulsed, and her pussy spasmed out of control.

"Great gringats!" the Beast exclaimed. "Are you all right?"

"Y… yes. Don't stop. Move me to the next one!"

The light jumped to the neighboring stone penis. The Beast yanked Red off her current rock lover and smashed her onto the next one.

"Oh my goddess! I'm a rock whore!" The sudden un-impaling and re-impaling sent uncontrollable vibrations through Red's slutty body. She was used to taking big cocks but not used to taking different ones so quickly one after the other. It was like a bunch of ogres were passing her around in a circle, piercing her tiny pussy and then tossing her onto their friend's huge cock. That was a scenario she now very much wanted to come true.

The Beast scurried back and forth, following the light pattern, constantly raising Red up and down on different sexy stalagmites.

After completion of the first sequence, the lights moved faster and in a different order, jumping from one rock cock to another one much farther away.

The Beast used his animal speed to fly back and forth between them. This meant Red was impaled much more swiftly. And was reduced to a moaning mess much more easily.

She flopped around like a rag doll, fully under the Beast's power. Her pussy became his sex toy, smashing down on whatever huge cock the cavern commanded. It was true there had been many times in her fuck-filled life she had felt like a sex toy, but never to this degree. Her pussy's sole purpose in life had become a hole to be plugged by gigantic stone cocks. What a noble purpose!

Her juices flowed down each stone edifice, her orgasms coming fast and hard after several circuits. Her eyes rolled to the back of her head. Her tongue hung out of her mouth. She was lost in helpless nirvana.

"Red, do you wish me to stop?" the Beast asked in concern.

"N... no," she managed to eke out. "P... please keep going!"

He did. Until the entire shaft of each stalagmite was covered in her cum. Only then did the next door open, proving Red was a worthy slut to advance farther into the horny cave.

The Beast pulled Red off the last stone cock. She glopped out one last round of cum, then huddled against his chest. He held her in his arms, cooing gently into her ear. She closed her eyes and smiled. He could be very sweet when he wanted.

"L… let's go into the next chamber," she said breathlessly.

"Very well. But then you will rest before tackling the next challenge."

"Okay," she replied. "That sounds nice. As long as you keep holding me."

"It would be my pleasure."

He carried her like his bride across the threshold of the next chamber. This one was larger and had two natural skylights in the stone roof.

Those skylights highlighted two impressive statues in the center of the room.

One was of Erus, the god of lust. He had massive stone pecs and an even more massive stone cock.

The other was of Tela, goddess of desire. She had the nicest rock-hard boobs Red had ever seen and a super-sexy stone pussy.

"What do these statues have to do with the next test?" the Beast wondered.

Red didn't wonder at all. She knew exactly what they had to do.

"We need to fuck that god and goddess!"

It was time for some heavenly sex!

Chapter 11

"We can't fuck statues!" the Beast protested.

"Sure we can! I'll hop on that big stone cock and you shove your huge beast into that goddess's tight cunt."

"That seems most improper."

Red put her hands on her hips. "You didn't think it was improper when I was just fucking all those huge stalagmites."

"Er, no, that was quite enticing."

She poked him in his furry chest. "Don't be a hypocrite, Beastie. Don't you think I want to see you ram a sexy goddess?"

"You do?"

"Sure. It'll be hot! Plus, I'm doing this to help you break the curse. You need to contribute to the fucking."

He sighed. "I suppose you have a point."

"I always have a point when it comes to sex!" Red dragged him over to Tela.

The Beast fidgeted, gazing at the voluptuous statue, which was just as tall as he was.

"What's wrong?" Red asked.

"We have not been properly introduced."

Red rolled her eyes. The Beast apparently liked being especially formal when it came to goddesses. "Okay, Beast, this is Tela. She's got huge tits and a super-juicy goddess pussy. Tela, this is Beast. He has super-cozy fur and a huge beastly cock!"

"That is not the proper way to introduce people," the Beast sputtered.

"It's the way I introduce people."

"You are a most inappropriate girl."

"I'm also a girl who's going to let you fuck her for two days straight in any hole you want."

The Beast's cock grew rapidly. "Er, perhaps you are not so inappropriate after all."

Red smiled. "Okay, let's get this goddess nice and wet!" She snatched the Beast's penis and yanked him forward.

He yelped. "Red, please be careful how you handle my, er…"

"Huge beast cock?"

"Yes, that."

"Sorry, I'm just excited to see you penetrate this crazy tight pussy." Tela did indeed have a narrow slit, which made sense. The goddess of desire should have the tightest pussy in the heavens. One that squeezed penises so strongly they were completely captive to her womanly wiles.

The Beast examined the stone vagina. "I do not think I will fit inside."

"We just need to tease her a little, get her nice and wet."

"How can I statue get wet?"

"She's a goddess. She has otherworldly powers."

The Beast grunted, indicating he didn't put much stock in

that. But he allowed Red to rub the tip of his cock up and down the granite lips. "Uhhhh, I… I did not realize statues could be so enticing."

"Oh yeah, they can be a lot of fun."

The Beast cast a sidelong glance at her. "Exactly how many statues have you made love to?"

"What? Oh, not that many. Maybe a couple dozen."

"Two dozen?! How have you been locating all these stone edifices?"

"I travel all over, and there are a lot of intricately carved statues. So, naturally, they need to be fucked."

"Naturally," the Beast replied sarcastically, his cock twitching against the goddess's pussy.

Tela's lips parted, sucking in the tip of the Beast's penis.

"Good god!" he exclaimed.

"Good goddess, you mean," Red corrected. "So she does have a magic pussy!"

"What should I do?" he asked.

"Ram it in her and give her a good goddess fucking!"

"Ahhh!" he groaned. "I don't know if I have a choice. She's pulling me into her." The Beast lurched forward, clasping Tela's shoulders as his cock slid fully inside.

"Damn, that is one greedy goddess!" Red exclaimed. "No wonder she's my favorite deity."

"Her pussy has clasped tightly around my penis," the Beast told her.

"Great! That means she wants you bad. Start thrusting!"

The Beast hesitated, his furry cheeks turning red.

Red threw up her hands. "What's wrong now? You have the hottest goddess in the pantheon begging you to fuck her."

"It is rather embarrassing with you watching."

"Aw, c'mon, I let people watch me get fucked all the time."

"That's because you are an incorrigible slut."

"Thank you!" Red glanced back at Erus's huge stone shaft. "Okay, I'll go fuck the horny god while you take care of this horny pussy. Then we can watch each other fuck. Sound good?"

"Uhhhhh!" the Beast moaned. Obviously, the Tela statue was squeezing him again, getting impatient that her pussy wasn't being hammered. She was quite needy for a statue. But everyone needed sex, so she had her priorities straight. "Th… that is acceptable."

"Great! But grab her ass when you fuck her. She'll like that." Red moved his paws from Tela's shoulders to her rock hard butt. If the goddess was like Red, she would love having her booty fondled while being fucked.

"My goodness!" the Beast exclaimed. "She's squeezing my dick even more forcefully."

Red hopped up and down. Yes! She knew Tela was a girl after her own heart. "Fantastic! Have fun with that pussy while I tend to a god's juicy cock." That was a sentence Red didn't get to utter very often. She wondered if she'd ever get to make love to a real god or goddess and if it would be as otherworldly as she imagined. Well, she would just have to prove she was the biggest slut who'd ever lived and Erus and Tela would appear to reward her for spreading their sexy gospel.

She scooted over to the nearby male statue. It was much larger than her. Its huge shaft pointed up at the perfect angle to be ridden.

Red leapt up, wrapping her arms around Erus's neck and her legs around his thighs.

"Hi, I'm Red." The Beast was right that it was only proper to introduce yourself to a deity before having sex. "I really like your cock." Erus didn't reply, but Red thought she felt the stone penis twitch underneath her.

She kissed him on his stone lips. "I'm going to be your little slut and fuck you as much as you want. Oh, and I'll scream super-slutty things and just be an all-around huge whore." This time she definitely felt the cock move. In fact, it grew upward, pressing against her already wet lips.

"Ooh, you like that huh? I thought you would. The Beast really likes it when I'm a big slut too. Right, Beastie?"

Her muscular and furry companion was ramming Tela's pussy so hard Red thought he might break the stone. "Uhhhhhhhh, y… yes, you are a wonderful slut!"

She smiled and turned back to Erus. "See? I've got the Beast Slut seal of approval! Now let's get this big dick in me."

She slid down his hips and instantly tensed as the tip of his stone penis entered her. "Ohhhhh fuck, that's big!" She clung to him as she lowered herself bit by bit, trying to adjust to his hugeness.

"N… no wonder girls become your whores so easily," Red told him, sliding past the halfway point of his girthy godhood.

Erus wad known to seduce all women he encountered, ravishing them and giving them the most epic orgasms they had ever experienced. Even though this was just a statue of the god, Red hoped it would provide her with similar orgasmic bliss.

She gasped loudly as she hit the hilt of his sexy sword. His stone cock was grooved perfectly to hit all her sensitive spots. She wiggled around, trying to get used to his girth. She was glad she had recently taken the Beast multiple times. It was definitely helping her take this god cock.

But Erus didn't want to wait. His arms moved toward her, his stone shoulders grating loudly as they rotated, and his hands grasped her hips. He had large fingers, which easily reached her ass.

"Oh my!" she gasped. "I didn't know you could move."

His only response was to raise her up, so only the tip of his penis was inside her, then bring her crashing back down on his full length.

"Holy shit!!" she screamed. "I'm being fucked by a sexy statue!"

"As am I!" the Beast roared. Tela had taken after her fellow deity, grabbing her lover's beastly buttocks and smashing his cock into her pussy extremely hard.

Red wondered how these statues were able to move. Maybe the gods themselves had imbued them with fucking powers to satisfy horny explorers. Or maybe a sneaky witch like Celestine cast some naughty magic on them. Either way, Red loved that the statues could take an active role in fucking her and the Beast.

Erus slammed her up and down on his slickening shaft. Slick because Red was leaking out plenty of her girl juices. She clung to her god lover, helpless to do anything except let her pussy be treated like Erus's fuck toy.

He went faster and faster. Red's moans got louder and louder.

"Ohhhh shit, gods really know how to destroy pussies!" she wailed, feeling like she was going to let loose a whole bunch of squirt-filled orgasms.

Next to her, the Beast was pounding the goddess's pussy at unnatural speeds. "Uhhhhh!" he moaned. "She's incredibly tight and keeps sucking me into her. I can't stop smashing her goddess vagina!"

While it was incredibly hot watching the Beast smash a sexy statue, Red didn't want him to get too enamored with the slutty goddess, who was obviously trying out-do Red in being a huge whore. Well, the goddess had met her match with this human nymphomaniac!

"Take my slutty pussy!" she screamed to Erus. "Smash it like it's your property. Don't stop fucking me until I've flooded the cavern with your cum and promised to be your sex slave for eternity!"

That really inspired the statue. Its stone hands moved so fast they were almost a blur. The sheer speed and power were nearly too much for Red. Her eyes lulled back into a state of semi-consciousness, orgasms ripping out of her, juices shooting everywhere. Her lips slipped off Erus's hips, her arms off his neck. She flopped around like a doll whose whole purpose was to be fucked by a god.

"Red, are you all right?" she vaguely heard the Beast ask.

"C... can't... s... stop... c... cumming," she managed to get out as she slipped in and out of consciousness.

"Hang on," he replied. "I'm coming! Gods, am I cumming!" He roared loudly and thrust particularly hard into Tela. "Take my seed, goddess!" He let out an orgasmic growl and emptied his balls into the stone pussy. He shot load after load into her until her arms sagged and her vagina finally released him.

He toppled backward onto his rear end, where he unleashed one last impressive salvo, coating Tela's tits and face. Red was happy she flitted into consciousness to see that. She knew the goddess would prove to be a real slut.

Erus still hadn't gotten enough of her pussy. It was flattering he was so obsessed with it. But Red didn't know how much longer she could hold out. Maybe mere mortals weren't meant to fuck gods.

"This pussy is mine!" the Beast roared, prying Erus's hands off Red's hips and yanking her off his drenched cock.

She and the Beast toppled to the floor. She landed on his huge chest, releasing the rest of her cum across his fur.

The Beast held her protectively as she trembled and came. She did it for a long time. But he never let go. His warmth and strength made her feel safe. She drifted off to sleep, still spilling her sweet juices.

She didn't know how long she had slumbered. But when

she woke, she was still in the Beast's arms, his fur matted by her sexy fluids.

She gazed into his blue eyes and kissed him. "You saved me."

"Of course. I will not let anything happen to you."

She snuggled into him. "And to think I started off as your prisoner."

"Yes, well, perhaps I can let you off for good behavior."

"More like naughty behavior," she replied, rubbing her breasts against his chest.

"Did that amorous god injure you?"

"No. It was actually amazing. I just wasn't prepared for how fast and hard it would be."

"Indeed. The goddess was also a very vigorous lover."

"Guess there's a reason they're the lust and desire deities."

The Beast nodded. "Do you think we quenched their sexual desire?"

In answer, another stone passageway opened.

"Yes!" Red cheered. "Our fucking powers are so good, the gods approve! Isn't that great?"

"Er, yes, wonderful. Are you fit to continue? Hopefully, the pommerac will reside in the next chamber."

"And hopefully we can do a lot more fucking!" Red hopped up, showing she was indeed fit.

The Beast sprang to his feet. "I thought Erus had made you sore."

"Ah, I got over it. I have a very quick sexual recovery time. Now let's go!"

She yanked him toward the doorway, excited to find the fucking fruit or just more things to fuck.

This was proving to be one sexy adventure!

Chapter 12

Red and the Beast entered the chamber. There weren't any stalagmites or statues to fuck. Just a hole in the far wall, about waist-height and with a diameter of about thirty-five inches.

Red rushed over to it and peeked inside.

A large purple pommerac, magically glistening, rested in a small alcove a few feet past the opening.

"Beast, look!" She yanked him down to the hole. "We found it!"

Her lover gazed inside, his furry cheek brushing her face. It tickled her pleasantly. He was so soft she would gladly cuddle up against him every night in his castle, making sweet love and drifting off to sleep in a cocoon of beastly love.

"I can't believe it truly exists," he marveled.

"I knew it was real," Red replied.

"How could you be so certain?"

"Sexy magic items are always real. What other reason is there to use magic than make people have fantastic orgasms?"

The Beast furrowed his brows. "There are many other reasons to use magic."

"Really? You should meet this witch friend of mine. She's really good at fucking me with her magic."

Her companion's eyes got even larger than their already

huge size. "I would like to meet this witch."

Red nudged him. "So you can watch her fuck me up the ass with her sexy wand?"

"What?! That is not what I meant."

"Well, it should have been what you meant."

He studied her for a moment. "Does she really use her wand to do that?"

"Oh yeah. She shoves it in my ass and pussy and totally dominates me. I'm pretty much her sex slave when she does that."

He stroked his furry chin. "I never thought of using a wand in that way."

She clasped his arm. "You gotta start thinking more sexy like me."

"If this pommerac does what you claim, I believe both of us will be able to think of nothing but sexy things."

"Yes! Won't that be great?"

He drank up her nude body. Her cloak had been abandoned outside the cave entrance after her initial stone penis fucking. "It will certainly not be arduous to make love to you countless times."

Red hugged him. "Aww, Beastie." It may not have been the most romantic ode ever, but for him, it was pretty good. And, quite frankly, Red didn't need sappy romantic stuff to convince her to have sex. She was always ready to fuck. Though she did appreciate her partners going the extra mile and being lovey-dovey, and she always rewarded them with an extra deep and long blowjob.

Red turned her attention back to the opening in the wall. "It's pretty tight, but I think I can fit." She nudged the Beast. "Hey, that's what you said the first time you saw my pussy." She giggled uncontrollably. Red was always good at amusing herself, usually by shoving her fingers in her tight folds.

"I most certainly did not say that," the Beast harrumphed.

"Aww, c'mon," Red pouted. "So you don't think I have a tight pussy?"

"Er, no, you do. It is actually the tightest I have ever felt. I meant I merely thought those words rather than said them out loud."

"I knew it!" Red stroked his cheek with one hand and his cock with the other. "You're getting the fucking of your life when we get out of here."

The Beast licked his lips. "Then let us make haste."

"Right!" Red stuck her arms through the hole, followed by her head. But then she had a problem. "Ack, my boobs are getting stuck on the bottom."

"That's because they are extremely large," the Beast helpfully informed her.

"Thanks! But can you smush them up so I can squeeze through?"

"I will try." The Beast enveloped her tits in his massive paws. Red tingled all over. She loved how he could feel up her entire chest with his large hands.

He moved her breasts left, right, back and forth, trying to find the best position to allow Red passage through the hole.

"Hey, are you trying to help or just feel me up?" she asked.

"I am trying to help. It is not easy. Your breasts are ridiculously firm."

"I'm loving all these boob compliments! But I was also hoping you were feeling me up."

"I will massage your breasts as much as you like later. We must get you to that pommerac."

"Right. Okay, just push them against my body as hard as you can."

"Are you sure? Won't that hurt?"

"Probably. But it will just be for a second. And I'm sure it won't hurt as much as all the huge cocks I've had in my ass recently."

"I thought you enjoyed anal sex."

"Heck yeah, I do! It's a pain-pleasure thing. You get used to it, and then it's real fun!"

"If you say so. Prepare yourself. I am going to massively contort your breasts."

Red prepared herself for massive contorting. "Ohhh shiiittt!" she yelled when the Beast pushed hard, flattening her melons against her body as much as possible.

He pushed forward at the same time and was able to pop her breasts through the opening.

"It worked!" he exclaimed.

"Yes!" she replied. "But, owww, my boobs are so sore."

"My apologies. I did warn you."

"It's not your fault. But I'm totally taking you up on that titty massage later."

"And you will have it. I always keep my word."

Red smiled. She liked that he was an honorable Beast.

She wiggled forward, moving more of her body through the opening.

But then she had another problem. Her hips, which were quite curvy, got stuck. "Arrgh, not again!"

"You are much too voluptuous," the Beast commented on the other side of the hole.

"Hey! Most people love my voluptuousness. Is that a word? Well, what I mean is, people enjoy my juicy booty!"

"I certainly do," her beastly paramour replied.

"Woohoo! Boob and butt compliments. This is one great adventure!"

While she celebrated, she gazed at the pommerac, just out of reach in the tiny alcove. She couldn't see the Beast because he was on the other side of the wall but she heard him do something very unusual. He was laughing. Or more like a guttural guffawing.

"What's so funny?" she demanded.

"The only thing I can see from this side is your butt wiggling around," he replied. "It is quite amusing."

Red scrunched up her nose. Stupid Beast laughing at her. But she supposed the fact that she was stuck in a tiny hole with her ass sticking out was pretty funny.

"I thought you liked it when I wiggled my butt," she said, wiggling it even more.

"I do. It makes me want to do this." He slapped her ass.

"Oww! Hey!"

"I am merely giving you your punishment for sneaking

into my castle."

"I thought being imprisoned was my punishment."

"I let you out very quickly. So you still need discipline."

Red smiled. The Beast was getting kinky. She was obviously rubbing off on him. But she wanted to keep playing along. "No fair! I'm totally helpless in this position." She wiggled around some more, showing exactly how stuck she was.

"Yes. It is excellent that you cannot pull any of your shenanigans. You must take your spankings like a proper slut."

"But I'm a very improper slut."

"Then you will get even more spankings." He whapped her ass again.

"Oh fuck, that's so hard! Please give me more!"

The Beast was happy to oblige, smacking her jiggling ass again and again with his strong paw. It was the hardest Red had ever been spanked, and it was really turning her on. Her pussy rubbed against the edge of the opening with each blow, making her nice and wet.

She was now happy she got stuck halfway through the hole. Being in a helpless position and getting spanked made her feel extremely submissive.

"Ohhh fuck, Beast! Spank me! Spank me like the naughty slut that I am!"

"I am very happy to spank naughty sluts," he replied, growling with each sinful smack.

Red's pussy was so wet she thought she might cum just by

getting her ass whacked. "Please fuck me, Beast! Fuck my tiny, slutty pussy!"

The Beast abruptly halted the booty discipline. "What?! You wish me to fuck you while you're stuck?"

"Yes! What better time to fuck a slut than when you have free reign over her ass and pussy?"

"But how will that help us get the pommerac?"

"If you smash my pussy hard enough, it will hopefully force me through the opening."

"This sounds like more of your unique Red logic."

"My unique logic is never wrong!"

He made a dismissive noise that told her what he thought of that statement.

"Hey, it's your fault for making me so horny with all your sexy spankings. Just look at how wet my pussy is." She was now dripping onto the floor of the cavern, so it was impossible for him to miss her state of arousal.

"Very well," he agreed. "It is hard to resist after seeing your rear end shake so deliciously."

"My rear end is very delicious!" She shook it for him a bunch more.

He grabbed it and placed the tip of his cock against her lips. They spread for him, having gotten to know his huge dick well.

He thrust fully into her, burying his shaft in her cozy cunt.

"Ohhh yesss!" she cried, thrilled to have his beastly cock once again filling her.

The sounds of his thighs slapping against her ass carried to the other side of the wall, where Red flopped around, dangling from the tiny opening.

"By the gods!" the Beast roared. "How can any pussy be this tight?"

"Oh fuck, Beast!" Red screamed in reply. "You're going to make me cum when you say things like that."

"I am going to be the one cumming before long. But I do not seem to be dislodging you."

Red moaned. Oh right, that was the point of the vigorous fucking. Red was enjoying it so much she almost forgot why they were there. "Fuck me harder! Pound me as hard as you can!"

"Are you certain?"

"Oh goddess, so certain!" she wailed, needing his Beast cock to fill her for eternity.

"Very well." He slammed her so powerfully, bits of dust fell from the wall. He was so strong. And so deep in her pussy. Deeper and fuller than she ever thought her tightness would be filled.

"Ohhhhh fuucckkk, Beast! I'm your slut! I'll be your sexy maid, your fuck toy, whatever you want. Just fill me with your creamy cum!"

Oh boy did he fill her. He erupted inside her, his bulbous dick expanding and releasing a huge stream of stickiness. He unloaded his seed into her like he hadn't cum for six months.

He wasn't the only one spurting. Red squirted her goodies all over his cock and thighs, her hips attempting to do sexy gymnastics but couldn't due to the tightness of the opening in the wall.

After several minutes of filling her, Red knew the Beast was almost done. "Pull out and dump the rest on my ass," she requested.

He did so, dribbling his cum over both her cheeks.

"Ohhh yeah," she cooed. "Just like that." A proper fucking always ended with her partners depositing their remaining cum on her ass.

Red dripped the Beast's cum out of her overfilled pussy. She hoped he was watching, turned on by how he overloaded her womanhood and made her his slut.

"Th… that was most stimulating," he panted. "But you are still stuck."

Red would happily be stuck all day if it meant the Beast would keep fucking her like that. But they did need to get the sexy fruit. Curse her hips being so much wider than her tiny waist. Actually, scratch that. Her curvy hips and butt were what got her laid so much. Her big tits probably didn't hurt either. So they just needed to figure out another way to free her.

And Red knew exactly what that way was.

"Okay, that was the right idea," she told the Beast. "We were just using the wrong hole."

"Wait?" he asked in shock. "You mean you wish me to…"

"Yup. Fuck my tight little ass!"

The Beast clasped her butt, and Red shivered.

It was time for her to take the largest cock she had ever had up her tiny back door.

Chapter 13

A ridiculously huge cock pressed against the ridiculously tiny opening of Red's ass.

"Oh goddess!" Her entire body tensed, preparing for her ass to be violated in ways it never had before.

"Red, are you sure you want to do this?" the Beast called from the other side of the hole, where Red's curvy butt was stuck.

"Yes! We need to get that pommerac. And I've been dreaming about you butt fucking me since the first time I saw your big beast."

"You have?"

"Oh yeah. I want to prove I can take more huge cocks up my ass than any other slut."

"That is a strange life goal."

"Hey! It's a perfectly reasonable goal. If you're a slutty sex maniac."

"You certainly fit that description."

"Thank you! Now are you going to ram my tight ass or what?"

"Yes. But I will begin slowly, so you can get used to my girth."

"Good idea. Your beast is enormous!"

"Perhaps I should lubricate it first," he suggested.

"Great! Use my pussy juice. I'm really wet down there."

He rubbed her slit, making her even wetter, and coated his paws in her juices. "You are very good at providing lubrication," he told her.

"Yup. I'm one wet slut!"

"Now, let us attend to your ass." He placed his forefinger against her opening.

"Ohhh fuck," she groaned. "That's a big finger."

"I am a big beast."

"You sure are!" she replied, picturing his huge cock. She wished she could see it, see it twitching in anticipation of penetrating her ass, dripping with the cum that he would assuredly shoot into her tiny cavern.

His finger parted her ass cheeks.

"Ohhhhh!" she gasped, the familiar zolt of slutty electricity shooting through her, something that always happened when she experienced that first anal piercing.

He worked farther in, making her moan deliciously. His finger was as big as some creatures' penises. Though it was nothing compared to the huge salami he was going to shove in her back door.

The Beast rested his paw on her butt while he kept exploring her delicious derrière. "I thought I would never experience anything tighter than your womanhood, but your rear end puts everything else to shame."

"Uhhhhhh!" she groaned. "Y… yeah, my butt's the sluttiest part of me."

"I'm having trouble getting my finger all the way in. I am concerned that my penis will not fit."

"I'm fitting it in my sluthole no matter what!" Red retorted. When people told her she couldn't do something sexually, it just made her determined to prove them wrong. She was going to take his huge cock in her tiny ass. Even if it made her want to be his ass fuck toy for the rest of her life.

"Very well," the Beast gave in, sliding his finger fully into her.

"Ohh yeah," she gasped. "That's the stuff! Wiggle it around inside me."

He did so, loosening her butt up and getting it ready for his beast of a cock.

"Hey Beast," she called back, dangling from the hole. "Do you like how I'm completely helpless and at your mercy?"

"Yes," he replied, thrusting his finger in and out of her and making her gasp several times. "Just like when you were in the castle cell."

"You are really obsessed with me being your prisoner. Ohh, I get it. It's one of your kinks."

"It is not one of my kinks," he protested.

"Okay, when we get back, I'll be your sexy prisoner as much as you want. As long as you promise to fuck the shit out of me in the cell.

He increased his finger fucking. "Perhaps it will become one of my kinks after all."

Red smiled. She was very good at introducing people, and Beasts, to new sexual activities.

"I think my butt is loosened up enough," she told him after a couple more minutes of delightful probing.

"I believe you are right. Your ass is greedily sucking up my finger."

"It will be even greedier with your dick. Let me have it!"

He let her have it. He rubbed his cock along her pussy, coating the tip in her girl juice. Then pressed it against her ass.

Red groaned loudly. His cock was way too big. Her ass struggled to open enough to allow him entry.

He kept a constant forward pressure, his penis ordering her ass to open further, open more than it ever had before.

After a few minutes of trying, her ass finally surrendered, knowing that it had to submit to the juicy cock, that it was helpless under its manly, or beastly, power. Red was proud of her butt. It knew when to step up and be the ultimate sluthole.

The Beast's head penetrated her. She tried to gasp, groan, utter something, but the sensation was so overwhelming all she could do is contort her face in sheer submissiveness. From the first inch of penetration, she knew her ass belonged to the Beast. That she was fully under his power and would agree to whatever sexually decadent thing he wanted. Of course, on a normal day, Red was up for just about any sexually decadent thing. But with a huge Beast cock in her ass, all bets were off. She was going to become the Beast's ultimate fuck toy.

"Ohhh go... goddess, Beast!" she cried when she could finally utter words from her throat. "My ass has never been spread like this before."

"And my cock has never been squeezed like this before,"

he replied with a horny growl.

To prove his point, Red's ass sucked in another two inches of his cock. Now that it had a taste of his hugeness, it needed more.

The Beast was ready to give it. He seized her hips and pushed into her.

"Uhhhhhhhhhhhhh!" Red groaned to the heavens. How could anything be this big? How could she have never had something like this in her ass before? And how could she convince the Beast to fuck her slutty butt every hour of every day?

He throbbed within her, like he was on the verge of exploding.

"Beast! Don't blow already. You just got inside me."

"I… I am trying not to. But I have never experienced anything like the sensations your ass is providing."

Red let out a happy moan. She was glad her booty was getting the Beast's stamp of approval.

"Well, I've never had a cock this massive in my ass before. And I want a full butt fucking from it. Then you can fill my ass with your seed as much as you want."

"I believe I will overflow your posterior with my semen."

"Yes, please!" Red loved it when her partners shot so much into her it flowed back out. It made her feel like a cum receptacle. Like a real fucking slut.

The Beast continued to push farther and farther into her, making Red squirm more and more.

Her ass was screaming at her, telling her she was crazy to

let something so big inside. But at the same time begging her to let the Beast shove it all the way in. Her ass was a complicated slut.

The decision was easy for Red. Of course she was going to let the Beast completely fill her tiny channel. "Ohhhh fuck, Beast! Please shove it all the way in. If you do, you'll turn me into your anal sex toy for life. I won't be able to resist you anytime you penetrate my booty. I'll turn into the most submissive whore you've ever seen!"

There was no way the Beast could hold back after hearing that. He plunged fully into her. She screamed. She cried. She begged for more. In short, she became the most submissive whore the Beast had ever seen.

He slammed her ass, lost in his animal cravings. Red's tears splashed the ground. It wasn't that it was too painful. It was just so much of an anal sensory overload, her body could barely process it.

She couldn't stop moaning, couldn't stop telling the Beast she was his butt slut, that she needed him to pound her even harder.

He went so hard that Red felt her hips begin to squeeze through the opening. "B… beast, it… it's working!" she groaned. "Fuck me as hard as you can!"

"Uhhhhhhh!" he growled. "I will obliterate this ass!"

"Goddess, yes! My ass deserves to be obliterated!"

Red didn't think it was possible to be pounded as hard as the Beast worked her ass. She was barely able to stay conscious. She had thought she had experienced all anal had to offer in her previous trysts. But the Beast was showing her a whole new world of ass dominance, a whole new level of ass sluttery she could aspire to.

Her hips kept inching forward. And, finally, with one last thrust that set off his climax, the Beast propelled Red through the hole.

His initial salvo filled her ass, but after she landed on the floor of the tiny chamber, the rest of his cum shot through the hole and splashed across her back, ass, and thighs. And he had a lot to shoot. Her ass had been so tight it seemed to have set off an especially huge orgasm within him. Red was so exhausted from the butt fucking she could do nothing but lay there and take it. Which was fine with her. She loved getting covered in her lovers' sticky juices.

"Ahhhhhhh!" the Beast yelled. "I cannot stop cumming!"

"Don't!" Red called back. "Cover me in your beast sauce!"

"As you wish." He shoved his dick through the hole and continued to spurt. Red took it like a good slut, her ass continuously expanding and contracting, like it was having trouble returning to its usual diameter after having something so huge in it.

When he was done, she had an inordinate amount of cum on her. She felt sexually linked to the Beast. It was as if the intense anal had formed an intense bond between them. A bond where she would be his sexy ass slut whenever he wanted.

He collapsed to his knees and peered through the opening. "Red, are you all right?"

"Y… yeah. Just really sore. Your big beast owned my ass."

"Is that a good thing?"

"It's a great thing! It means I'm going to be a huge butt slut for you!"

"Oh. That is good news indeed."

Red giggled. The Beast was so formal it was funny when he admitted how much he enjoyed ramming her ass.

She managed to get to her hands and knees and crawled to the alcove. She plucked the purple pommerac from its resting place. It was surprisingly warm and soft. It looked juicy, like it was waiting to be eaten. Just like her juicy pussy!

She crawled back to the hole and produced the pommerac. "I've got it!"

"Well done. You are an intrepid and resourceful young woman."

"Thank you!" It was true: Red was very resourceful when it game to sexual matters.

"But how will you get back through the opening?" the Beast asked.

Red hadn't considered that. She was too focused on getting fucked out of her mind.

She tapped her lips. "I know! I'll masturbate really hard and smear my juices all over my tits and hips. That will lubricate me enough to squeeze through."

"An excellent idea," the Beast replied, licking his lips.

Red smiled. "But I need a little break after all that ass fucking. Stick your dick through the hole."

"What?! How will that help you rest?"

"I just need to rest my pussy and butt. My mouth is fine. And we need to do something to pass the time."

"There are many other things we could do, like discuss fine literature or the beauty of nature."

"Yeah, yeah, we can do that back at the castle. Right now, I want to suck your cock!" That got the Beat to rise to full mast. He stuck it through the opening, and she immediately took it in her mouth.

"Mmmm," she murmured, loving his musty taste. There was still a bit of post-cum on his tip, which she eagerly licked up.

She held on to the rocky opening and sucked the meaty member until the Beast exploded. She squealed as he flooded her mouth, but she didn't let go. She kept her lips plastered around his cock, gulping him down.

"Uhhhhhh, Red," he groaned. "Your mouth is a wonder!"

She tried to thank him, but it wasn't easy to talk with a huge cock in your mouth.

She gasped when she finally released him, her hands taking the place of her mouth on his penis as she aimed it at her face to make sure his last few spurts covered her cheeks.

"See, wasn't that fun?" she asked.

"Y… yes," the Beast panted. "Very fun."

"You know what will also be fun?"

"Watching you manipulate your womanhood?"

"Yes!" she replied. "You're totally getting it!" She was so proud of him for learning her sexy ways.

She remained on her knees, her butt still too sore to sit on, and spread her legs. She rubbed her slit and then was two fingers deep, fucking the shit out of her pussy.

"Ohhhh fuck! Beast, do you like watching me play with myself?"

His large eyes peered through the hole. His mouth was open, salivating at the scene before him. "It is a very enjoyable activity."

She grabbed her left tit with her other hand, massaging her nipple. "Good. It really turns me on when you watch me. I like performing for you." She pounded her pussy harder, wanting to put on a squirt show for the Beast.

"You are an extremely adept performer," he said.

"Ohhhhh, thank you. You know what will help me perform even better?"

"What?"

"You telling me what you want to do to me."

"You mean assist you in getting out of this cave?"

"No, silly. Like what you want to do to me sexually. It will help me cum if you make me feel like a slut."

"Oh, er, well, I... um, would like to insert my penis in your vagina."

"Beast!"

"What?"

"That's like the most unsexy way to say it."

"Well pardon me. I am not used to this type of naughty dialogue."

"That's okay. I'll teach you. Tell me you're going to ram my pussy so hard you'll turn me into your personal whore who only exists to be filled with your beastly cum."

"I cannot say that!"

"C'mon, please. It will make me squirt extra hard. Don't you want to give me a nice orgasm like I gave you?"

"Well, it is honorable to return favors like that."

"Great! Then tell me what a slut I am!"

"Er, you are the biggest slut I have ever seen. I am going to pound you. Um, I mean pound your pussy into whoredom and overflow it until you are dripping in my cum."

"Ohhhhh fuck, Beast! Yes, that's it! I want to always be dripping in your cum. I want your cock to dominate my mouth, pussy, and ass!" Red fucked herself as hard as she could, using her other hand to rub her clit raw.

"Um, I will be happy to do that. I will shove it in every hole you have until you learn what a proper slut you are."

Red was so close to cumming. She just needed one last push. "Yes! Yes! I want to be a proper slut! Please order me to cum. I can't climax without your permission!"

"Really?" The Beast was surprised to know he had that much power over her. "Very well, since you have proven to be such an epic whore, you may cum."

"Ohhhhhhhhhhhhhhh!" she screamed, squirting her juices everywhere. "Thank you! Thank you for letting me cum!" Red would have cum anyway, but the fact that the Beast gave her permission made her climax even more spectacular.

She rinsed her hands in her waterfall, wiping her juices across her tits and hips. She kept cumming, making sure she lubed up her most pronounced assets as much as possible.

"You have very impressive orgasms," the Beast said, unable to take his eyes off her writhing, squirting body.

"Th… thanks," she moaned, continuing to lather herself up.

After she flooded most of the small chamber, she clambered back into the hole. The Beast grabbed her from the other side and yanked her forward. Her boobs popped through fairly easily and her hips only got suck a little before slipping through the tight opening. Her cum was an excellent lubricant.

She was so exhausted from all the fucking she could barely stand. She stumbled forward. The Beast caught her and swept her into his arms.

"I will carry you," he told her, cradling her against his powerful chest.

She clutched the fruit to her bosom and buried her face into his furry warmth.

He made his way back through all the chambers and was able to use his animal agility to scale the slope they had tumbled down.

They emerged into daylight, the sun having completed over half its daily journey in the sky above.

The Beast draped Red's cloak over her naked body and strode back toward the castle.

Red snuggled against him, feeling safe and content.

She drifted off to sleep, dreaming of how the horny pommerac was going to turn them into non-stop sex machines.

She couldn't wait.

Chapter 14

Red woke in a comfy bed. She rubbed her naked body along the silk sheets, loving how they felt against her skin.

She didn't remember how she wound up in the bed. Usually it was because of fun sexy times. But she definitely would have remembered that. She never forgot any time she got fucked.

She recalled getting the pommerac and the Beast carrying her out of the cave. She must have drifted off after that, and her lover must have brought her all the way back to the castle and tucked her in. What a sweet little scruffball he was.

She also noticed her body was free of the boatload of cum that had adorned it during their journey. Aha, he must have bathed her too. She must have really been passed out if she slept through all that. But that's what a beastly butt fucking will do to you.

She smiled, imagining the Beast's gentle paws soaping up her nude body. So he was a sweet and naughty little scruffball. Red's favorite kind!

She slid out of bed and stretched, testing how her body was feeling. Pretty good it turned out. There was only a slight lingering soreness in her tush. The rest of her was raring to go.

As soon as she exited the bedroom, she was greeted with a

wonderful smell: bacon, eggs, and sausage.

She hurried down the large central staircase and scooted into the kitchen.

There, the Beast stood over the wood-fired stove, frying eggs in a pan. He wore a light blue apron that was much too small for him.

Red tried to suppress a giggle. "Aw, you look adorable."

He turned to face her, revealing the frilly white trim along the apron. Even more adorable!

"You are finally awake," he stated. "I thought you might sleep all week."

She stretched again, glancing out the window at the morning sun. Oh wow, she *had* slept. It was still light out when they had left the cave, so she must have snoozed the rest of the afternoon and through the night. "Hey, when you get your ass rammed by a huge Beast, it really tires you out."

"Are you still sore?" he asked with concern.

"Just a little. But don't worry, I'm fit for more fucking!"

He smiled and returned to cooking. "That is good news."

"Yup. It's also good news you're making breakfast. It smells delicious."

"I am glad to hear it. I enjoy cooking."

Red smiled. She wouldn't have guessed that about the strong, serious Beast. But appearances weren't everything.

"But since I'm your maid, shouldn't I be doing that?" she asked.

"I decided to give you the morning off since you were so exhausted."

"Ooh, you're such a nice master. Hey, what's this?" She plucked her bra and panties from the table.

"I washed and sewed them last night. I felt bad about ripping them off you."

Red's jaw dropped. The Beast could cook and sew? And he had soft fur and a huge cock. Red wondered if she had met her dream mate.

She hugged him from behind, peppering kisses along his soft coat. "That was so sweet. Thank you!"

"Red, you almost made me ruin the eggs," he complained as she jostled him.

"Why don't you fry those eggs on my ass?" she replied, grinding against him. "It's pretty hot." She giggled, once again amusing herself.

"I will spank your ass if you keep making those terrible jokes."

Red raised her eyebrows. "Promise?"

The Beast rolled his eyes. "Would you please let me finish cooking?"

"Sure thing!" She plopped her shapely bottom on a chair and twirled her panties around her finger. "I do appreciate you fixing my underwear, though I won't need them while I'm here."

"Why is that?"

"I decided to be fully naked for the rest of my stay."

"Oh really?"

"Yup. It's only proper for house guests to repay their hosts by prancing around nude and letting them fuck their slutty bodies."

"I have not heard of that form of payment before."

"Oh it's really effective. It's how I get most of my lodging."

The Beast sighed. "You are incorrigible."

"An incorrigible slut? You know it! But right now, I'm your incorrigible slut."

The Beast glanced back at her. She had her long legs crossed, her arms folded under her bosom, pushing up her already impressive breasts.

"I am happy to hear that," he told her. "All right, breakfast is ready."

"Yay!" Red snatched plates, cups, and silverware from the Beast's cabinets and set the table as he brought over mountains of food. Being a huge Beast, he probably had a huge appetite. That was good. Red loved to eat and also loved working food into sexy bedroom activities.

Red dug in. "Mmm, this is so good. You're an excellent chef."

"Thank you. When you live by yourself, you must learn to do many things."

Red put her hand on his paw, feeling a tinge of sadness at how long he had been alone. "Yer ot ong eny mrr," she said with her mouth full.

"What?"

She swallowed. "Sorry. I said, you're not alone any more."

He gazed at her with his bright blue eyes. Eyes that began to water. "Thank you, Red," he said before quickly getting up. "Let me get us more food."

Red smiled. She knew he was embarrassed for her to see him show emotion. Which he didn't need to be. But she would let him get comfortable with that in his own time. She was just happy her words meant so much to him. And more food was a good idea. The Beast had already wolfed down several pounds of meat, and Red was ready for seconds too.

They sat, ate, and chatted, laughing at Red's silly jokes.

Then they did the dishes together, Red rubbing her hip against the Beast's thigh. He splashed soapy water across her breasts. She retaliated and they were soon both very wet, though not in the usual way from their sexy exploits.

They dried off and then warmed up by the fireplace in the Beast's study.

Red sat on his comfy lap, resting her head against his chest and stroking his fur. She let out a contented breath, watching the fire crackle, feeling its warmth against her naked skin, and listening to the Beast's strong heartbeat.

"Thanks for carrying me back from the cave," she told him.

"It was my pleasure."

"And for bathing me."

"Er, yes, I hope you do not mind. You were very sticky."

She snuggled into him more. "Not at all. Did you touch me anywhere naughty?"

"Of course not! Well, that is, I had to at certain times to get you fully clean."

"Beast! You're so scandalous."

"I most certainly am not. It was just, you had the most, er, stickiness on your breasts, buttocks, and vagina."

"Hmm, I wonder how that happened."

He looked down at her. "Are you teasing me again?"

"Yup. It's one of my favorite activities."

"That activity is very annoying."

"Well, one of my other favorite activities is sucking your huge cock!"

"That activity is very enjoyable."

Red giggled. She thought he would say that.

She patted his chest. "And don't worry. You have permission to touch me wherever you want. When you bathe me or any other time. I like having your hands all over me."

"You do?"

"Fuck, yeah! You have a very sexy and gentle touch."

He wrapped his arms around her. "I am glad to hear that."

They sat by the fire, snuggling and smooching and enjoying each other's company.

Red was so content she didn't want to move. But she knew she had an important, and sexy, task to complete. "Do you want to eat the pommerac now?"

"Perhaps you should rest some more," he replied. "Your pussy and ass took many rammings yesterday."

"Did they ever! Especially by your huge, delicious cock!" She felt that cock grow hard against her thigh. "But I'm ready for more. I committed to helping you, and that's what I'm going to do."

He brushed her cheek with his paw. "You are an honorable woman."

"And a horny woman!"

"Indeed. Those qualities make for a potent combination."

Red kissed him, glad he was becoming as smitten with her as she was with him. "So, ready to get started?"

"I, er, still feel it might be better to wait."

"What? Don't you want to break the curse?"

"Well, yes, but, um… that is…"

She studied him, realizing he was embarrassed to reveal the truth. "Beast, whatever it is, you can tell me. And since we've shared so many intimate moments, it's part of the Laws of Horniness that you must reveal all secrets to me."

"There is no such thing as the Laws of Horniness," he retorted, trying to hide a smile.

"Sure there is. I just made them up."

"Very well. I will tell you."

Red beamed. These horny laws were working way better than she expected.

"I'm hesitant to eat the pommerac," he told her. "Because, well, I… I know once the curse is broken you will leave and I will never see you again."

Red's eyes watered. "Oh, Beast!" She straddled him and grabbed his face, giving him the deepest kiss she could muster. He enveloped her in his arms, his large tongue filling her mouth, swirling with hers. It was one of the most passionate kisses Red had ever experienced. And she never wanted it to end. Never wanted to leave the Beast's arms.

"It won't be the last time you see me," she said, stroking his cheeks. "I really care about you."

"You do?"

"Of course, silly. You're a furry little sweetheart."

"I am not sure if thats the best description for me," he harrumphed.

She ruffled his fur. "Yes it is. Because under all your gruffness, you're kind, noble, and courageous."

The Beast smiled, obviously pleased to hear such praise from her.

"Plus you're an expert at slutting me up with your huge cock!" she added.

He rolled his eyes. "You never stop, do you?"

"Nope. But, seriously, I want to spend a lot more time with you. Why don't you come with me after we finish all the fucking?"

"You would want me to accompany you?"

"Sure. It'd be an exciting adventure of fun and fucking!"

He licked his lips. "That is very enticing." His hands moved down her back to her ass. "Would I get to play with your posterior as much as I wanted?"

"Uh huh."

"And your womanhood?"

"Uh huh."

"And the rest of your beautiful body?"

"You can do whatever you want to every sexy and naughty part of me." She kissed him again and moaned into his lips as he squeezed her ass. There wasn't anything quite like two big Beast paws on your rear end to make you feel like a sexy slut.

"Thank you, Red," he said, gazing into her green eyes. "I

am glad I met you. And am sorry I imprisoned you."

"Oh, don't worry about it at all. It was sexy imprisonment, so it was right up my alley."

He smiled. "You are a remarkable woman."

She wiggled on his lap, coaxing his little beast into activity. "Ooh, you're so full of compliments now. I like it! And it's making me horny. Let's eat that sexy fruit and fuck for two straight days!"

"Your enthusiasm is contagious," he replied. "I am ready to dominate your pussy and ass."

"That's the spirit!" she cheered.

He snatched the purple fruit from the stand next to the chair.

They both eyed it, like it was some mystical artifact. Which, well, it was.

"Who should take the first bite?" he asked.

"I will!" Red volunteered. "I'm the biggest slut here, so it's only right I'm the first to suck on some horny fruit."

"I cannot dispute your logic," the Beast replied.

Red smiled. Few could argue when she used slutty logic.

She took the oblong pommerac from him and brought it to her mouth.

She took a bite. It was sweet and acidic, a tangy combination.

At first, nothing happened. But then she felt a tingle in her pussy. A tingle that spread to her ass, hips, thighs, breasts, and every other part of her. A tingle that rapidly grew to an overwhelming sensation. A sensation that was telling her she needed to be fucked. Telling her that her whole purpose in life was to fuck. Fuck, fuck, and fuck some more. Never stop fucking. Never stop cumming. Never stop until she became the ultimate sex machine.

And that's exactly what she was going to do.

Chapter 15

Red ate half of the fruit, then shoved the remainder into the Beast's mouth. She normally would have been more delicate about it, but she didn't have time for that. She needed to be fucked. Fucked harder than she ever had in her entire life.

She couldn't believe the horny powers of the pommerac had taken hold so quickly. She squirmed on the Beast's lap, needing him to plow her pussy.

He gobbled the pommerac, his eyes gleaming with a hungry sexual intensity. His erection grew in an instant, parting Red's lower lips as it expanded.

He yanked her hips down as his cock shot up, impaling her with his huge beast.

"Ohhhhhh fuck, Beast! You're even huger than all the other times you've been inside me!"

He let out a sexual growl, licking her breasts and clasping her hips. "I... I think it is the powers of the pommerac. I have never felt so horny before."

"Me either! And I'm always horny!" Red was shocked there was something that could top her already extremely high libido. But the fruit had at least quadrupled her desire to be fucked. It was all she could think about. All that mattered in the entire world.

She grabbed his arms as he slammed her up and down on his cock. He was so powerful, he had complete control over her body, her pussy turning into his plaything.

"Ohhhhhh fuuuuuuccckkkkkk!" she cried. "Ram my pussy like I'm your fuck toy! Your horny, helpless fuck toy!"

He rammed her. And rammed her. And rammed her some more. Until their screams reverberated throughout the castle.

He shot his seed up into her, and she spilled hers down upon him. Their orgasms were even stronger than usual, likely due to the power of the sexual fruit.

They shuddered in each other's arms as they climaxed, lost in their mutual passion.

The Beast went flaccid after emptying his huge balls, but a second later, was fully erect again. And fully filling Red's pussy.

"Oh goddess, Beast! You're so hard inside me!"

"Y… yes, it seems the pommerac is living up to its name, letting us make love non-stop."

"I love this fruit!" Red screamed. "My pussy feels ready to go another hundred rounds!"

"I think it will be even more than that," the Beast replied. "I can think of nothing but how much I want to fuck you."

"Yes!!!" Red cheered. She loved it when her partners couldn't think of anything except how much they waned to fuck her.

The Beast stood, took a few giant strides, and pressed Red against the wall next to the fireplace. She wrapped her legs around him and let him go to town on her.

He pounded her so hard, the room shook, candles falling off the mantle above the fire.

"Uhhhhhhhh!" Red moaned. "My pussy belongs to you!"

"Yes!" he roared. "I want your pussy. I want it more than anything and never want to let it go!"

Red tingled all over. She wasn't sure if it was just from the powers of the pommerac or from how much the Beast desired her. She hoped after the fruit's horniness wore off, he would want her just as much.

"Ahhhhhhhh! I'm going to cum again!" The Beast pressed his body even further against her, his furry manliness enveloping her.

"Yes, Beast! Please cum inside me! Fill me with your seed! I want to take all of it!" While Red normally uttered super-slutty stuff like that during sex, she realized she was coming off even more desperate than usual. The pommerac had turned her into a sex machine, where the only purpose of her pussy was to be a cum receptacle for the Beast.

Luckily, she was getting to shoot her juices just as much. She squirted past his huge cock while it pumped his creamy fluid into her.

The next thing Red knew, she was on her back on the rug in front of the fireplace, the Beast on top of her, pinning her to the floor while he impaled her over and over.

Red clung to him, never wanting to be apart from his muscular body, never wanting his cock to leave her pussy.

"R... Red, I... I cannot stop making love to you."

"I... I can't either! But that's good, right? That's how we can break your curse."

"Y... yes. But are you really all right with fucking for two days straight?"

"Fuck yes! I'll make love to you for a week straight. Your body is so warm and cozy. And your cock's the greatest gift to man, er, beastkind."

The Beast blushed while continuing to thrust into her. "Er, that is... quite complimentary."

"Ohhhh fuck, that's deep!" Red squealed, proving how amazing his cock was.

"Your pussy is the ultimate gift!" he replied.

"Yes! Say more nice things about my pussy while you fuck me!"

That really got him going. He increased his gyrations, forcing Red's thighs open as far as possible. "Um, well, your pussy is the tightest thing I've ever been inside."

"Yes!" Red shrieked, undulating her hips in time to the Beast's thrusts. "More!"

"It grips and massages my cock like nothing I could imagine."

"Oh fuck, you're making me so hot, Beast!"

"And it squirts so much delicious nectar it's as if you are a goddess."

"Ohhhhhh Beast!!!" Red was so moved by his ode to her pussy she instantly squirted her nectar for him. Squirted it all over him, the floor, and herself. If her pussy had been aimed at the fireplace, she would have extinguished the flames with her flood.

The Beast carried her up to one of the towers of the castle, throwing open the shutters as he bent her over a stone windowsill.

"I need it in my ass!" Red cried. She loved all the attention he was giving her pussy, but her ass was getting jealous. It needed to be pounded into oblivion. Luckily, that's exactly what he did.

He yanked her arms behind her while smashing her way-too-tight ass. Red loved anal, but she had never craved it like this before. Her ass greedily sucked him inside, squeezing around his bulbous, throbbing cock like it never wanted to let go.

"I'm getting fucked up the ass by a huge Beast!" she screamed out the window. She was a big proponent of announcing to everyone when she was getting fucked out of her mind. She wasn't sure if the woodland critters enjoyed hearing her sexy moans. But any humanoid creatures in the vicinity probably did. She hoped she inspired them to fuck as hard as she and the Beast were going at it.

The Beast wrecked her ass. But in the best possible way. He made Red feel like the biggest butt slut in history. Like her ass always needed an oversized cock inside it.

He came particularly hard this time. Red knew her ass always made him spew the most, something she was quite proud of. He flooded Red's tiny hole so much he had to pull out and wound up shooting the rest over her head and out the window. If anyone happened to be standing underneath, they would have gotten quite a surprise. Of course, Red loved surprise cum facials, so she wouldn't have minded at all. Just like she didn't mind the Beast dribbling the remainder of his cum across her ass cheeks.

He spun her around, bringing her pussy once again onto his erect shaft. She had never seen the Beast so forceful. He was taking what he wanted. And right now, he wanted Red's dripping wet pussy.

He clasped one arm around her and leaped out of the window.

"Holy shiiiiittttt!" Red screamed. Both from the deep penetration she was receiving and the sudden free fall.

The Beast springboarded off parapets and ledges, traversing the exterior of the castle like he was a monkey in the jungle.

When he landed on the ground, Red was forced fully down onto his cock. She let out the longest and loudest scream yet, her cum unleashing across the grass and dirt.

She snatched the Beast's fur, her body held up by his cock, her feet dangling in the air. "O… oh goddess, Beast. You've dominated me more than anyone ever has. I'm yours forever!"

"Good," he replied, cradling her to his body and swirling his cock inside her. "I want you forever."

Red trembled. "Oh Beast, you're so domineering!"

"I am sorry, Red. I cannot seem to contain myself."

"No, it's amazing. I want you to dominate me."

"Excellent. Because I want to fuck you while you're wet."

"I'm so wet for you, Beast!"

"Er, yes you are. But I meant I want to make love to you in the river that runs next to the castle."

"Oh, gotcha. Make me overflow the banks of the river with my cum!"

He ran toward the meandering body of water, Red bouncing on his dick the entire way. She moaned and came, hoping the Beast would take her jogging like this more often.

He splashed into the water, submerging his body up past his furry belly button.

Red squirmed as he fucked her underwater. The only parts of her above the surface were her head and breasts, which bounced loudly against the crystal-clear stream.

"Red, you are a sexual goddess!" he growled.

"That's the nicest thing anyone's ever said to me!" she squealed.

He thrust into her again and again, her womanly virtue mixing with the river.

"Let's kiss underwater while we fuck," she suggested.

The Beast dipped them below the surface. They pressed their lips together, their passionate embrace providing all the oxygen they needed.

They both came underwater, their orgasms forcing them to exhale in a throaty scream, which forced them to surface, where they shared their climatic delight with the rest of the mountain.

The Beast carried Red out of the water. They fell to their knees on the bank, both taking a brief respite.

Red looked at the Beast's drenched body and giggled. His

damp fur made his face saggy and his body shriveled. Though the most important thing on him wasn't shriveled at all: his cock still stood at full attention.

"What is so funny?" he demanded.

"Nothing," she replied, trying to get her giggle fit under control. "I'm just not used to seeing you soaked. Besides soaked in my cum of course."

"Yes, you are very good at that." He got on all fours and shook his body like a dog, spraying water all over Red.

"Ahhhhhh!" she shrieked. "Beast, you're getting me all wet!"

"You cannot possibly get any wetter than you already are."

"That's true," she replied with a grin, massaging her soaked pussy lips. "Ready to get back at it?"

His throbbing cock answered for him.

"I wanna be on top this time." She straddled his hips and sunk onto his meaty shaft. "Ohhhh fuck, I missed this cock!"

"You were only away from it for a minute."

"That's way too long! I need your big beast inside me every minute of every day!"

"As you wish." He snatched her hips and smashed her up and down on his dominator. With every thrust, she was reminded of how much she was his slut. Of how much she needed his cum filling her pussy and ass.

They kept fucking outside the castle: in bales of hay, among the branches of trees, and over the blacksmith anvil he kept in a workshop next to the castle.

As they were heading back to the main entrance, Red

sitting on the Beast's cock while he carried her, a group of people approached.

The Beast turned toward them, presenting Red's naked ass for all to see.

"Ohhhh," she moaned. "Good idea, show them how slutty I am." She was so overwhelmed with passion from the pommerac and the Beast's lovemaking, she didn't care how many people watched her get her pussy pounded. The more the better!

"I... do not think they are here to observe our frolicking," he replied, continuing to pound her.

"There he is!" one of the villager's cried. "He's attacking that poor girl."

Red glanced over her shoulder. Oh shit, the Beast was right. They weren't here to be voyeurs.

"We could hear her screams all the way down in the village," another one of the townsfolk said.

Red cried out loudly to prove their point. She couldn't help it. The way the Beast's cock filled every last inch of her made it impossible not to scream. Though she was slightly embarrassed her cries of pleasure had carried that far. That was a new record for her. Ah, fuck being embarrassed. That was something to be proud of!

A third villager stepped forward. "We can't let him make a whore out of this innocent girl."

Red would have told them she was far from innocent, and she was already a whore well before meeting the Beast, but she was too busy moaning. As was the Beast. Their lust had completely overtaken them, so all they could do was fuck. Which was a problem, since they couldn't explain to the villagers what was really going on. They were too busy crying out in climatic bliss.

Apparently, the villagers still thought Red was in danger. The first one to speak pointed his wooden staff at them.

"Kill the Beast!"

Red's eyes widened. They had to fight off these villagers while fucking.

Damn, her pussy got her into a lot of trouble.

Chapter 16

The Beast bolted from the angry villagers, Red bouncing on his cock.

"Ohhhhhh fuck, I'm cumming so hard!" she screamed.

She left a trail of her juices behind them as the Beast dashed into the castle.

The villagers were hot on their heels, chasing them into the grand foyer.

The Beast swung Red in a circle. She kicked several villagers, knocking them onto their butts. Then he deposited her back on his cock.

"Ohhh fuck, that's better!" She promptly came again.

The Beast tossed Red around like an acrobat. She landed punches and kicks to more of the villagers who tried to reach them with their makeshift weapons.

Each time, he would bring her back onto his throbbing cock, making her cum. Red had never had a sex fight like this, but she was loving it!

He hurled her like a cannonball at two approaching townsfolk. She planted one foot on each of their chests, kicking them to the floor. As she did, she propelled herself backward, did a flip, and landed perfectly onto the Beast's pulsating penis.

"Oh goddess, I'm cumming again!"

"As am I!" he concurred.

She squirted across the carpet, her feet dangling off the ground, held up only by his massive cock. He, meanwhile, pumped his seed up into her.

"Let's use our cum as a weapon," she suggested.

"What do you mean?"

"Take me off your yummy cock and I'll show you!"

He removed her from his erupting appendage and set her on the floor.

She snatched her clit, directing her salty squirt gun at the villagers. She had pinpoint accuracy with her pussy, nailing several of them in the eye with her cum.

"That is most impressive," the Best commented.

"You can do it too." She grabbed his cock and pumped it hard, aiming it at more of their attackers. He sprayed over ten feet across the room, blinding several opponents.

"We're so good at cumming!" Red beamed.

"I've never had a woman handle my cock like you!" He continued to spew, unable to resist Red's tantalizing touch.

"Thanks! I'm an expert cock handler."

"Let's use their momentary distraction to our advantage." He tossed Red high into the air.

As she reached the peak of her upward journey, feeling weightless, she watched the Beast move like lightning through the crowd, upending villagers and tossing them across the room.

He dispatched the last of them just as Red came back

down. He positioned his cock underneath her, and she landed right on it.

Dropping that far onto a ridiculously huge cock was something beyond what even a super-nympho like Red had experienced. The force of the impaling vibrated her entire body. Her ass shook like it was the epicenter of an earthquake. Her arms and legs flailed out of control. And she came. Came like never before.

She gushed like when the sky cast down its torrential waters. She flooded the foyer, creating a pool of her sexy juices that crept past the dazed villagers sprawled on the floor.

Her landing had a similar effect on the Beast. He erupted into her, overflowing her tiny pussy, his semen gushing out alongside her less viscous juices.

The townsfolk stared at Red's undulating body, at the non-stop flood pouring out of her. And then tore their clothes off.

"Let's fuck!" one of them cried.

In the blink of an eye, a huge orgy filled the foyer.

"Yes!" Red cried between orgasmic moans. "We've inspired everyone to have sex!"

The Beast continued to thrust into her, spilling more and more of his thick semen. "I suppose that is one way to win a battle."

"It's the best way! Now overflow my tight cooch!"

He did so, pouring so much into her that when he lifted her off his cock, she spent several minutes expelling all the cum he had left inside her.

"Ohh fuck, Beast! No one has cum inside me that much before."

"My cock cannot resist your tight womanhood," he replied.

"Great! Now let's go join the orgy."

"What?! But those people wanted to eliminate me a moment ago."

"Yeah, but now we're all sexy friends. And by fucking them, we'll become best friends."

"You have a very strange logic. Is this how you make all your friends?"

"Pretty much. It's how we became friends, right?"

"Indeed. You are a hard woman to resist."

"That's what I like to hear. Now ram me from behind while I eat out that cute redhead."

The Beast tossed Red onto her knees and did her doggy, or Beast, style, while Red attacked the crimson bush before her.

The girl had a tangy sweetness to her, and Red made sure to lick her until she got a proper facial.

She moved among different villagers, wanting to fuck as many as possible. The Beast kept his residence in her pussy. She couldn't be apart from his delicious cock for more than a few moments. But she sucked plenty of other salamis and ate out lots of cute cooches while he pummeled her slutty pussy.

After two hours of fucking, the villagers were spent. They ambled off toward their homes. Red had pleasured all of them so well, their anger had dissipated. Plus, watching her beg the Beast for his cum convinced them he was in no way harming her. They realized a slut of her stature was in heaven with such a wonderful Beast cock filling her.

Red waved goodbye to them as her lover smashed her up and down on his shaft. He had fucked her so much while standing, her feet hadn't touched the floor in a while. She had never been with a partner so strong that he could manipulate her body at will. And boy did the Beast manipulate it: he pretzeled her in all different positions, seeing which ones allowed for the deepest penetration. Red loved experiments like that. And she loved having her legs twisted in ways that made her feel submissive and helpless.

"Ohhhh, how long have we been fucking?" she asked as the Beast pressed her against the huge castle door and fucked her from behind.

"I… I have lost track," he grunted.

"Me too! I can't stop fucking!"

"Neither can I! The pommerac is more potent than I could have imagined."

"Best fruit ever!" Red agreed.

He pummeled her until he came for like the five hundredth time. Then he took a brief respite, leaning his body against hers and pinning her to the door.

Red couldn't move. The Beast enveloped her. The only things keeping her up was his bulk and his very erect cock. She was buried on it up to its hilt and had no way down without his say so.

"Ohh Beast, I… I feel so helpless."

"Do you like feeling helpless?"

"Yes! I love it when you have total control over my body."

"So you would like me to continue ravishing you?"

"Fuck, yes! Ravish away!"

He ravished her all over the castle. His cock was constantly in her pussy or ass. His fur was constantly keeping her warm. His eyes were constantly gazing at her with a combination of lust and love.

"Fuck me in the cell!" she begged after her latest squirtfest in one of the towers.

"You wish to be my prisoner again?"

"Yes! Your slutty prisoner!"

The Beast carried her down the stone staircase, each step bouncing Red on his always hard cock. Red didn't think it was possible for a male to be rock hard this long, but that was magic for you. It could do wonderful things, especially when it came to sex. Just ask Celestine. She knew how to do orgasmically wicked magic.

The Beast jumped into the cell and closed the door, making it seem like they were locked inside.

He shoved Red against the bars.

She clasped them, sticking her butt out for him. "Chain me to the bars!"

The Beast placed manacles around her wrists and lashed them above her.

She squirmed around, trying to free herself. "Oh, you nasty Beast. You've tied me up and I'm completely helpless!"

"You wish me to untie you?" he asked, confused.

"No, silly, I'm just acting like your helpless prisoner. It

makes it more exciting."

"Ah, I see. What shall I act like?"

"The hunky jailer who loves disciplining naughty sluts."

"Well, you are a naughty slut, so I think I can play the role well."

"That's the spirit!"

He slapped her ass. "Why did you break into my castle?"

"I was hungry and wanted food," she replied in a whimper.

"So you are a thief? Do you know the punishment for stealing?"

"Is it lots of spankings?"

"Correct." He lashed out with fifty ass-quaking slaps. They were so forceful, Red came after every blow.

He gazed at the expanding puddle between her feet. "I see you are an especially epic slut. You cannot stop leaking."

"Ohhhhh, I'm sorry! Is there more punishment for being an especially epic slut?"

"Yes. You must take your jailer's full cock inside you."

"Damn, Beast, you're so good at this," Red commented, looking at him over her shoulder.

That got her another booty whap. "You are breaking character, Red."

"Oops, sorry! Please give me your huge cock, sir! I'll take it all like a good prison slut!"

He clasped her hips and parted her pussy lips with his big head. No matter how many times he entered her, that first sensation was always the best. It made Red tingle and gasp and anticipate the greatest fucking of her life!

He slid all the way inside her until he brought her onto her toes.

"Oh goddess, I never thought anyone could be this big! Are you going to fuck me every night in my cell?"

"Yes. As my prisoner, you are to be my personal fuck toy."

Red shivered. She loved roleplaying, and the Beast was surprisingly good at it. "Yes! I'll be your fuck toy. My body exists to please you!"

"You will make an excellent prisoner." He smashed her pussy until she leaked all over the cell and he leaked inside her.

"Red, your submissive demeanor is driving me wild!" he roared.

"Great! Your cock is driving me wild!"

He lifted her up enough so she cleared his cock and could release all the cum he had deposited in her.

"Oh sir," she said, getting back into character. "Is there any way I can earn my freedom?"

"Yes. You can let me spear your delicious posterior."

"You want to fuck me in the ass?" she asked, shocked. Of course, Red wouldn't have been shocked by that kind of request. She had experienced so many cocks in her ass recently she might as well rent it out at parties.

"Correct. You have the most enticing buttocks I have ever seen. And you are my prisoner, remember?"

"R… right. O… okay. But I've never done anal before. Can you please be gentle?"

"You are very talented at playing a coy, innocent lass," the Beast remarked.

"Hey, who's breaking character now? And are you saying I'm not innocent?"

The Best smirked at her, knowing full well Red had lost her ass innocence a long time ago.

"Please fuck me in the ass, sir!" Red cried as the naughty prisoner.

The Beast spread her cheeks and dominated her behind like no one else could.

Red's sexy prisoner persona instantly became an anal whore. "Oh goddess, I love being fucked in the ass!"

"Good," her jailer replied. "For I will do it multiple times every day."

"Yes!!!"

The Beast filled her ass with his cum, then untied her and ravaged her on the floor of the cell.

They made love for hours upon hours in the place they had first met.

Red lost track of the time. She didn't know how long they had been fucking. All she knew is she wanted nothing but to fuck the Beast for eternity.

Eventually, she passed out on top of him, his cock still inside her, his warm semen flowing into her.

Her hazy vision registered a magical glow around them before she lost herself fully to sleep.

She was sure whatever it was, it'd be fine.

Magic never went wrong, right?

Chapter 17

Red woke with a warm, juicy cock within her womb. Which was always the best way to start her day.

She rubbed her head against the soft fur underneath her and blinked her eyes open.

The Beast snoozed with his strong arms around her. He hadn't changed back to a human, even though they had fucked for two days straight, supposedly the way to break the curse put upon him.

Red wasn't disappointed at all. She thought the Beast was handsome just the way he was and loved snuggling into his furry body. Though she felt bad for him: he had waited a long time to break the curse.

His large eyes opened and gazed upon her.

"Hi!" she greeted him.

"Hello. How are you feeling?"

"Great! I had a nice Beast cock in my pussy all night long."

"I have never been inside a woman for that length of time."

"My pussy's pretty cozy, right?"

"Indeed. I could spend an eternity inside it."

"Aw, Beast, that's the nicest thing anyone's ever said to me." She would have smooched him on the lips but she couldn't reach due to being speared on his huge shaft. So she contented herself with peppering kisses along his furry chest.

He glanced down at his body. "It seems the curse has not been broken."

"Well, maybe it just takes a little while to reverse itself. Or maybe we have to fuck for a week straight!"

"You are very insatiable when it comes to sex."

"You bet I am!"

"I would not protest making love to you for that long."

"Is that your way of saying you want to ram my tight pussy more than any other pussy on earth?"

"Er, yes."

"Thanks!"

"But perhaps we should clean ourselves and seek nourishment before we continue."

"Good idea." They had been fucking for so long Red couldn't remember the last time she ate.

She pushed herself up, but her hips wouldn't move. "Um, I think we have a problem."

"What is it?"

"I can't get off your dick."

"That's ridiculous." He grabbed her waist and lifted. And then yelped as his penis was pulled upward with Red's pussy. "What in hades is happening?"

Red squirmed on top of him. No matter how she adjusted herself, she couldn't move one inch off his cock. She was stuck at the base of his sword, fully impaled by his wonderful monstrosity. "I don't know. Could it be part of the curse?"

Since there seemed to be some magical force holding Red's pussy around the Beast's penis, it wasn't that far-fetched of an idea.

"You mean we're stuck like this forever?"

"Geez, don't say it like that," she replied. "I thought my pussy was your favorite."

"I'm sorry, Red. I did not mean it like that. If I am to be stuck in any woman's folds, yours would surely be my choice. But we cannot go through life with my beasthood in your tightness."

"Are you sure?" She put her hands on his chest as she straddled him. "Your cock feels sooooo good inside me." She had spent so many hours with it in her womb, she had gotten very used to it filling her. It would almost be foreign to not have his cock inside her.

"Reddddd," he scolded.

"Okay, okay, I know, we have to find a solution. I just really like your cock." She wiggled on top of him.

"Uhhhhhh," he groaned, his penis throbbing within her. "And I greatly enjoy being inside you."

She wiggled more. "That's what I like to hear. And, you know, maybe it's just an after-effect of the pommerac."

"But when will this after-effect wear off?"

"Who knows? We'll just have to go around like this in the meantime."

"You seem to be taking this very well."

"I had a wand stuck in my ass recently, so I'm kind of used to it."

"You have had many sexual misadventures."

"You have no idea." Red thought back to Celestine's wonderful wand buried deep in her ass, making her feel like the biggest anal slut ever. "Oh, my witch friend can probably help. Or at least point us in the right direction."

"Where is she located?"

"I left her and Harry just outside of Honeydew."

"Honeydew?! That is several days' journey away."

"Yup."

"How can we travel there when we're stuck like this?"

"Easy. You just fuck me the whole way there."

"Red, you are being ridiculous."

"No, you're not being ridiculous enough." She beamed at him, knowing he couldn't resist her charm.

"Fine," he harrumphed. "But who is this Harry?"

"He's a headless horseman."

"A what?"

"A horseman who doesn't have a head. Well, he has a had but it won't stay attached, so he carries it around with him."

"You have very unique friends."

"Yup. I love unique people. Like you!"

He smiled. "You have excellent taste."

She giggled. "So, want to go wash off now?"

"Very well." He rose to his feet, and she wrapped her arms and legs around him.

He descended the stairs and exited the castle, his cock throbbing inside her the entire time.

"Ohh fuck," she moaned. "This is the best way to travel!"

"How does your vagina keep getting tighter?" he grunted.

"Um, I think your cock's just keeps getting bigger." Red would have liked to claim her cooch was constantly getting cozier, but she had to give credit to the expanding beast in her wet channel.

He waded into the lake and used the soap they had brought from the castle.

Red scrubbed the Beast's chest and face, making it look like he had a soapy beard.

She giggled. "You look good, Bubble Beard."

"What about you?" he retorted, slathering an inordinate amount of soap on her perky tits.

"Oh, you can call me Bubble Breasts anytime you want."

He smiled and returned to work on her body. Because of her smaller size and her position on his cock, he could easily clean all of her, except where he filled her pussy.

His hands roamed her buttocks, squeezing and spanking them.

"Wow," she remarked. "You really want to make sure my ass is clean."

"I like to be thorough."

She giggled again and cleaned around his dick and his huge balls.

He growled pleasurably. "You seem to want to make sure that area is clean."

"Yup. I'm an expert cock and balls washer." That was true, though she usually cleaned them with her mouth.

While it was somewhat awkward trying to bathe with the

Beast's cock stuck in Red's pussy, they managed to mostly get themselves clean.

The Beast dunked them underwater several times, even doing it as a surprise when all the soap was off, eliciting squeals of laughter from Red.

"You're a sneaky Beast," she told him affectionately, wet hair plastered to her face.

He gently brushed it behind her ears. "And you are a beautiful woman."

She kissed him. Long and passionately, loving the feel of his lips against hers and his cock against the walls of her pussy.

He carried her back to the castle, where they dried off and made their way to the kitchen.

Cooking was also a challenge with Red clinging to the Beast, but they managed to fry up some ham and eggs.

Red snuck in kisses while they cooked, thinking it was rather cozy making food together.

The Beast sat at the table, Red's ass cheeks jiggling on his lap as his cock rumbled inside her.

She fed him food, smiling at how he ravenously wolfed it down.

She sucked sensually on a mapleberry, letting it turn her lips red and licking the juices off them.

That made the Beast enlarge inside her.

"Ohhh Beast," she cooed. "Let's eat breakfast like this every morning."

He grinned, popping ham and more berries in her mouth.

They continued to feed each other, enjoying the warmth of their partner's body.

Red sighed, very content to be forced to snuggle with the Beast and have his huge cock inside her. She knew she should probably be more worried about it being stuck in her. But it felt so wonderful. And she enjoyed being in the Beast's arms, feeling his soft fur and his gentle breath. It certainly wouldn't be the worst thing in the world if she had to adjust to having his cock take up residence in her pussy.

When they were done eating, Red threw her arms around his broad neck. "Make love to me, Beast!"

He grabbed her hips, his fingers brushing her ass cheeks.

She rocked back and forth on him. She couldn't raise up much due to the magic holding her on his cock. But she managed to get a slight up and down motion going, as well as plenty of back and forth gyrations.

They kissed and made love, and he came gently inside her.

He massaged her clit with his thumb and made her join his orgasmic release.

They moaned into each others' mouths, enjoying their dual climaxes.

Red rested her head against his chest, trembling from the post-coitus bliss. Being stuck on his cock made her feel even closer to him. In a weird way, this was one of the most romantic experiences of her life.

They cleansed their bodies again and packed supplies for their journey, including Red's underwear and cloak. They wrapped the magic rose in cloth and placed it in the satchel.

Red hoped it could help Harry.

She remained naked for their travels. If she was going to have a huge Beast cock inside her, wearing clothing would just be silly.

They kept mainly to the forests to stay out of sight. The Beast would normally attract attention on his own. He certainly would with a sexy slut attached to his dick.

Red bounced on the Beast's cock with every stride, meaning her pussy was constantly filled with wonderful sensations that made her want to completely submit to him.

"Ohhh Beast," she remarked a couple of hours into their journey. "I feel like I'm going to cum with every step you take."

"Yes. I think I will be filling you many times before we reach our destination."

"Heck yeah! Fill me with your Beastly cum until I can't take it anymore!"

He increased his stride, making her moan louder.

Red had decided this was the only way to travel from now on when she heard a familiar raspy, high-pitched voice.

"Lookie lads, it be our favorite human slut!"

The six goblins she kept running into emerged from the trees, cocks at the ready as they eyed her jiggling ass.

She sighed. Guess she had a bunch more butt fucking in her future.

Chapter 18

"Hey goblins!" Red greeted them warmly. "How've you been?"

"Much better now dat you here," their leader replied.

Red smiled. The goblins were weird, but Red loved how much they desired her body.

"You know these creatures?" the Beast asked.

"Yup. We're good friends."

The chief goblin nodded his head. And his cock. "Oh yah, we best friends. Best fucking friends."

"You let goblins penetrate you?" the Beast asked incredulously.

"Of course. They have juicy dicks. I also let a big Beast penetrate me. Over and over again."

"Oh, well, that is different."

"Bestie, you're not saying goblins are too strange are you? Don't some foolish people say that about you?"

"Er, yes."

"And isn't that frustrating?"

"Very much."

"So we should be accepting of goblins too." She smiled at him, wiggling on his throbbing cock.

He sighed. "You are right. Your acceptance of others is a

wonderful quality to emulate."

"So you're saying I'm the most wonderful girl in the land?"

"Yes."

"Woohoo! I love Beastie compliments!" She kissed his chest and squeezed his cock with her pussy.

"Red, if you keep doing that, you're going to make me spill inside you again."

"That's the idea!"

The goblins hopped up and down. "Gud idea. We spill inside ye too."

"Sorry, boys. My pussy's reserved for the Beast right now. I'm kind of magically stuck on it."

The small creatures nodded like that was a totally normal thing to hear. "Dat okay. We like fucking yer ass de best."

"Yah," another agreed. "It be yer best sluthole."

"It made for goblin cum!"

The Beast frowned. "These creatures are most uncouth."

"Yeah!" Red echoed. "Do you goblins think you own my ass?"

They looked at each other, then back at Red. "Yah."

She rolled her eyes. Of course they did. Well, with all the times she let them probe her back door, she really couldn't blame them. "Well, okay, but only because I like you guys so much."

"Yah yah yah! Yah yah yah!" The goblins did a weird goblin dance, their cocks bobbing and swaying. Red was almost hypnotized with so many cocks swinging back and forth.

"Are you really going to let them penetrate your behind?" the Beast inquired.

"Oh yeah, they've fucked my ass a whole bunch of times. They're really good at it."

"Yah," Chief Gobby said. "We gud butt fuckers, specially dis butt." He slapped Red's ass.

The Beast lifted him into the air with one hand. The goblin flailed, helpless against the Beast's powerful grip.

"You do not touch Red's succulent bottom without her permission," the Beast growled.

Red beamed. She loved that he thought she had a succulent butt and that he was defending her honor.

She rubbed his furry chest. "Beast, that's very gallant of you, but I don't mind them spanking me. You know how I love booty discipline."

"Yes. You are always very eager for spankings."

"Heck yeah! And these goblins are good spankers. They may seem weird but they can be also be sweet."

"Yah, see, we nice goblins," the dangling creature said. "We even nicer when we get to stick goblin cock in slut ass."

Red giggled. "They're a little obsessed with my butt."

The Beast placed his other hand on her bottom, rubbing it softly. "On that point, I agree with them."

He set the goblin down, putting his other hand on Red's ass.

She wiggled on his cock, loving how his paws felt. "Ooh, looks like someone wants my ass all to himself."

"I am merely massaging it to make it feel better after that vicious spanking."

Red smiled. She had taken way harder ass slaps than that. She prided herself on being able to take the hardest spankings anyone could dish out. So she knew the Beast was merely using that as an excuse to hog her booty. But it was sweet he wanted her all to himself.

"Don't be jealous, Beastie. My pussy still fully belongs to you."

"I am not jealous of goblins."

"Then you won't mind if they fuck me in the ass."

"Well…" He muttered something else incomprehensible.

"C'mon, wasn't it fun when you and the gringat fucked both my holes?"

"You were especially vocal during that."

"Yes! The more people fucking me, the sluttier I get. I promise if all these goblins fuck my ass while you pound my pussy, I'll be your sex slave whenever you want. And will give you the most amazing blowjob of your life!"

The Beast grew so large within Red's pussy, she squealed.

"I agree to this arrangement," he said eagerly.

Red smiled. She was very good at getting people to go along with her sexy plans.

"Dis great plan," the goblin leader said. "Let's fuck dat ass, boys!"

"Wait!" Red cried. "You know the rules."

"Oh, right. We lubicate first."

"You got it," she replied. At least they were learning.

She replaced the Beast's hands on her ass with her own and spread her cheeks. "Beast, can you make me cum?"

"With pleasure." He bounced her on his dick, and she was dripping over the goblins' fingers in no time.

They shoved their cum-coated fingers up her ass.

"Ack!" she squealed as three digits penetrated her. "One at a time."

"Ah, we sorry. We get excited when we see such hot ass."

Red sighed. She could never stay mad at the goblins when they said stuff like that. She never had any creatures adore her butt as much as these gobbies.

They probed her behind a whole bunch, opening it up so it was ready for their much larger cocks.

The Beast knelt to give the goblins better access to Red's ass.

The leader rammed his penis into her.

"Ohh fuck!" she cried, throwing her head back and getting a lovely view of the wispy clouds.

"Red, are you all right?" the Beast asked.

"Yup. I love getting both my holes fucked!"

"Me love fucking yer hole too." The goblin smashed her ass, which made her rock back and forth on the Beast's huge appendage.

She clung to her animal-like companion, stuffed beyond belief and beyond happy to have a Beast and goblin cock inside her.

"We love how her ass shake," the other goblins cheered. "Make it jiggle more."

Their leader happily complied, ramming Red so hard her ass cheeks rippled like a raging river.

"Ohhhhhh! G… glad you guys are enjoying the show." It excited her that they couldn't take their eyes off her ass. If she was ever free of the Beast's cock, she'd have to do a booty-shaking strip show for them. And then let them grope and fuck her as much as they wanted. Not that she was in any rush to get off the Beast. His cock throbbed warmly inside her, nice and snug in her tight cooch.

"Dis best show ever!" the goblins agreed, hopping from one foot to the other, as goblins were known to do.

The leader unloaded in her ass with a guttural goblin grunt.

"Goddess, you're filling my ass so much!" Red knew they loved hearing her slutty commentary.

"We'll see who can fill you the best." The Beast unleashed a torrent of his own cum into her channel.

Red squirmed from the dual flows, feeling overloaded by the sheer amount of semen squirting into her. "Oh Beast, your cum is stuck inside me!" His cock was acting like a stopgap, preventing his gift from fully leaking back out, thought some did seep around his meaty shaft.

"I'm sorry, Red. I cannot resist your pussy."

"Don't resist it! I love it when you fill me. I feel like I belong to you."

"Don't fergit, ye belong to us too." The goblin leader shot one last round into her ass, then let one of his comrades take over.

The second goblin immediately slid in all the way to his hilt and vigorously fucked her. These goblins never wanted to give her poor booty a break. Luckily, the forty-eight hour fuck-a-thon she had with the Beast had really improved her stamina. Her ass could take lots of fuckings and still be raring to go!

The goblins fucked her one after the other, each cumming inside her, while the Beast swiveled his always erect cock within her pussy.

The goblin brothers fucked her at the same time, both squeezing inside her ass. Receiving three different streams of cum made her feel particularly slutty. So she didn't object when the goblins wanted to go another round, all six of them taking another crack at her throbbing ass.

When they were finally done, her ass expanded and contracted, wondering if anything else would be shoved up it.

Red had lots of goblin cum along her back and booty and even more inside her. With that and the Beast's seed, she was one full slut!

"Tanks for de fucking," the head goblin said. "Yer still our favorite human slut."

"Hey, thanks!" Red took great pride in that. Goblins might be strange, but they had excellent taste in sluts.

"See ye next time. We fuck ye even harder then." They all gave her a slap on the ass and then tromped off into the forest.

"Goblins are very strange creatures," the Beast said.

"Yup. But do they ever know how to fuck a girl's ass!"

"And what about me?"

"Oh, you really know how to fuck a girl's ass too. When you're out of my pussy, you can ram me back there as much as you want."

"Excellent. I enjoy ramming you in many places."

Red smiled. "Hehe, I'm turning you into as big of a nymphomaniac as me."

"I do not think anyone can match you in that regard."

"Thank you! Now, onward to the sexy witch!"

They managed to make their way to the outskirts of Honeydew without running into any other goblins or other creatures who wanted to probe Red's ass.

Red directed Harry to the small inn where she had parted company with Harry and Celestine.

"We can't walk in like this," the Beast said.

"Why not?"

"For one, I am a Beast. For another, you're glued to my penis."

"Hey, you're a wonderful, handsome Beast. People just need to accept you for who you are."

The Beast smiled. "Thank you, Red, You are a kind woman. But what of the other problem?"

"I don't think they'll notice."

"What? They won't notice my Beasthood filling your delicious pussy?"

"Ooh, keep calling it delicious. That makes me really horny!"

"You are always horny."

"Well, even hornier!"

"Stop being so sexy or you'll make me cum inside you again."

"Great!"

The Beast sighed, probably wondering how he wound up with such a silly sexpot.

"Don't you want to find my witch friend?" she asked.

"Yes."

"Then stop worrying what other people think and let's go!"

"Very well."

He marched them inside the building, where the proprietress was sweeping the floors and two customers were eating.

They all gaped at the huge Beast and the curvy slut stuck to his cock.

"Hi, remember me?" Red said to the owner. "I was here with a sexy redhead and a rather stiff gentleman." When Harry had to balance his head on top of his neck, he had to walk very rigidly, thus the stiff description. Though his cock was nice and stiff too whenever he stuck it inside Red.

"Oh, yes," the shopkeeper replied. "You were wearing slightly more clothing then."

Red grinned. It was true her normal outfit barely qualified as clothing. "Yeah, this hunk of a Beast ripped them off because he couldn't wait to fuck me. Are my friends here?"

"Yes. They've been checking every day to see if you returned." The woman didn't seem taken aback by Red's confession of the Beast freeing her of her garments or that his cock was currently inside her. She probably knew a horny slut when she saw one.

"Great! Thanks so much. Let's go upstairs, Beast."

He remained silent and headed for the steps, nowhere near as comfortable with public nudity.

She bounced on his cock with every step until she couldn't take it any longer.

"Ohhh fuck, I'm cumming!" she shouted on the top step.

The shopkeeper and customers rushed over and glanced up to catch her orgasmic faces and her juices spilling down the stairs.

"Oops, sorry about the spillage. I'll clean it up later, promise."

"Oh, don't worry," the owner replied. "Your friends have been doing that all week long."

"What? They've been having lots of orgasms without me? How dare they!"

"Red," the Beast said. "May I remind you that you have been having sex with me, a gringat, and six goblins while you've been away."

"Oh, right. I guess it's okay then."

He rolled his eyes, obviously not understanding her horny weirdness.

They made their way down the corridor and opened the last door on the right.

And got quite a sight.

Celestine was tied up in the middle of the room, fully nude. Her arms were stretched above her, wrists bound with rope that was lashed to a beam near the ceiling. Her legs were spread wide, ankles tied to iron rings in the floor.

A headless man stood behind her, thrusting his huge cock into her drenched pussy. A pussy that had already sprung a leak for there was a large pool of cum beneath her.

Harry and Celestine were fucking.

And Red couldn't wait to join them.

Chapter 19

"Super-slut has returned!" Red announced to her two fucking friends, who at that precise moment decided to cum.

Harry's headless body tightened behind the sultry witch and unloaded his headless cum into her.

Celestine squirted across the room, splattering Red's ass. Which made Red very happy. It had been too long since the witch had coated Red in her sexy juices.

"I see where you get your nymphomania from," the Beast remarked.

"Actually, they get it from me," Red replied with a sexy smirk.

Her two friends finished cumming, though Harry stayed inside Celestine, making sure she knew who was boss. Even though the witch had been the dominant one when Red met her, Celestine secretly wanted to be dominated. Maybe not so secretly, since she appeared to be letting Harry do whatever he wanted to her.

"Red!" she exclaimed, her pussy still dripping. "We're so glad you're back."

"Yes," Harry agreed. His head was on a nearby chair, providing a good vantage to watch his body fuck the witch slut. "We were worried about your well-being."

"Aww, you two are sweet. I'm okay, except I have a huge cock stuck in my pussy."

"I thought you enjoyed my cock," the Beast said.

"Oh, I do. I love it! This is Beast by the way. And this is Harry and Celestine."

The Beast nodded. "It is a pleasure to meet friends of Red."

Celestine trembled from her post-orgasmic bliss, her witch tits shaking wonderfully. "You are the owner of the castle in Avinnois?"

"I am."

"No wonder people said you were such a beast in the bedroom."

"He sure is!" Red agreed. "He fucked me all over the castle."

The Beast expanded within her. "It was a very pleasurable experience."

Harry frowned, gazing at Red's pulsating pussy on the Beast's cock.

"But I love fucking you guys too," Red quickly added. "Harry, your cock makes me wetter than the seven seas, and Celestine, you make me a magical slut."

That put a smile on both her friends' faces.

"Speaking of." Celestine muttered some witchy words in a witchy language. Her wand floated across the room and inserted itself in Red's ass.

"Holy shit!" Her butt contracted around the foreign object, wanting to make it as hard as possible for the wand to enter, knowing that would make Red feel particularly slutty.

"Celestine!"

"Now, now, Red. It's been far too long since my wand's taken residence in your lovely bottom. Take it like a good slut. I'm sure the Beast knows how much you love having your ass filled."

He nodded. "Indeed, she requested many anal probings from me."

The wand forced its way in farther. Red clung to the Beast's fur. She had forgotten how well Celestine's magic wand could dominate her. "Fuck! Okay, I'm an anal slut and everyone knows it. Happy?"

"Yes," the Beast replied.

"Absolutely," Harry added.

"Extremely," Celestine echoed.

Red blushed. She hadn't realized her butt sluttery was that popular among her friends. Guess that meant she had to do even more anal. Sounded good to her!

"How did you get stuck on that lovely cock?" Celestine asked. That led to Harry giving her an extra thrust. "Uhhhhh, not as lovely as yours, my dear. Yours is the one I constantly want inside me."

That made Harry so happy he unloaded another round of cum into her.

Red smiled. Apparently, the two had put aside their past disagreements and had become close friends and lovers again. She liked it when people fucked instead of fought.

She was also impressed by how comfortable Celestine was talking to them while tied up, covered in cum, a huge cock in her pussy. She chatted with them like they were having tea downstairs in the tavern. Red could learn a lot from her older friend about being a confidant slut.

The Beast sat in the chair next to Harry. The motion made his cock and the wand vibrate inside her.

"Ooooh, that feels good," she cooed before turning to Celestine's question. "Well, it's a bit of a long story, but the gist is, we ate this magical pommerac that gave us amazing sexual stamina, but now his cock and my pussy seem to be fused together."

"Red!" Celestine scolded. "You should not experiment with magic you don't understand. I learned that the hard way."

"I know! But it was the only way to break the Beast's curse, which would help me get the rose to break Harry's curse, but now I'm the one who's cursed!"

"That is a lot of curses," Harry remarked.

Red sighed. "Tell me about it. At least this is a sexy one though." She wiggled on the Beast's lap, never tiring of how he felt inside her. It also reminded her how deep the wand was up her butt. She really liked having things in her ass. It was so comfy having a stuffed booty!

"But why did you need the extra sexual stamina?" Celestine asked.

"Indeed," Harry added. "You possess more natural sexual endurance than anyone I've met."

Celestine squeezed his cock inside her pussy, making him cum again.

"Uhhhhhhh!" he moaned. "Outside of you, of course, my sweet. Both you and Red are insatiable sluts."

"That's better," the witch replied, smiling down at his head.

Red grinned. There was obviously a bit of jealously any time Harry and Celestine complimented another sexual partner. Red would have been jealous herself, but fortunately she had gotten to fuck the Beast non-stop and become enamored with him. So she didn't mind that Harry and Celestine had swapped lots of sexy juices. Though she was still determined to prove she was a bigger, longer lasting slut than the sensual witch. She couldn't lose to someone fifteen years older than her, even though Celestine was at the height of her beauty. The young slut should probably learn all she could from the older woman. But she had a competitive slut-streak and was determined to top the witch. She also wouldn't mind getting on top of the witch and fucking her again.

"The sorceress who cursed me said I had to find a woman to fuck for two days straight," the Beast told them. "Otherwise, I would remain a Beast forever."

"Hmm," Celestine replied. "I have never heard of a marathon sex session breaking a curse. Are you sure the witch was telling the truth? We can be quite devious."

"Quite devious," the disembodied Harry head agreed.

"Dear, I said I was sorry. I'm mortified by what I did to you."

"I am merely teasing, you saucy witch. However, you still

need to be punished." He pulled out of her pussy, slapped her ass, then shoved his huge cock in her tiniest hole.

"By the goddess!" she shrieked. "Yes! I love how you punish me!"

Red gazed at Celestine's bound body, her long red tresses falling past her shoulders, her tight butt filled with a juicy cock. She looked radiant. "Wow, you've really let Harry dominate you."

"Yes," the witch agreed with the type of groan she only made when there was a headless cock up her ass. "He has gotten very good at taking command of my naked body. It's quite wonderful."

Red nodded eagerly. "I'll say. Rough ass fuckings are the best!"

"I am sorry to interrupt this fascinating anal discussion," the Beast said with a hint of sarcasm. "But are you saying Red and I spent forty-eight hours making love for no reason?"

"No reason!" Red cried. "Harry, that's so insulting!" Red prided herself on giving her partners the best sex of their lives. This was a severe blow to her sexy ego.

He ran his soft paw through her hair. "No, no, I did not mean it like that. I apologize. I have never had a more wondrous two days in my life. It was beyond anything I could ever imagine."

Red beamed. "Yay! That's more like it. I feel the same way. You were amazing!" She gave him a big, wet, beastly kiss.

Harry cleared his throat. "I'm not sure we need to hear all the details."

"Don't be jealous, honey," Celestine chided. "Remember, we were fucking non-stop while Red was gone. It's only fair that she have fun too."

Harry sighed. "You are right. I'm sorry, Red. I just miss our three-way trysts."

"Me too!" Red replied. "I know, all four of us should have a huge orgy, and then we'll all be fuck friends."

Celestine smiled. "Leave it to our favorite slut to think of a great solution."

"That's me! But you should talk, you tied-up witch tart."

"Witch tart?" Celestine whispered to her wand, and it vibrated powerfully in Red's ass.

"Ohhhh shit!" Red whimpered. "That's playing dirty. Harry, ram her ass!"

The horseman was glad to do so. He smashed Celestine's perky butt, making her moan as much as Red.

That turned the Beast on so much that he swiveled Red back and forth on his cock.

He and Harry came at the same time, the Beast filling Red's pussy, the horseman filling Celestine's ass.

"Ohhhhh, I love cum in my ass!" the witch screamed.

"Ahhhhh, I love it in my ass and pussy!" Red shrieked.

"Stop trying to outdo me, you little slut."

"I'm a bigger sex maniac than you, you witch whore." Red knew it was ridiculous to argue about who was sluttier, but it sure was fun!

"You are both huge sluts," Harry said. "Now take our cum and moan like good girls."

Red and Celestine moaned like good girls and took all the sticky cum their partners expelled. Harry was much more commanding than the last time Red fucked him. The witch must be rubbing off on him. Or he was becoming more confident in his domination of sluts. Good for him!

"That was very well said, my headless friend," the Beast told Harry. "Your mate moans almost as seductively as Red."

"What?" Celestine said, clearly insulted. "I can moan way better." She demonstrated, letting out a deep, throaty, sensual scream that made Red cum on the spot.

The young sexpot wasn't going to be outdone. "Oh yeah, how about this?" She let loose her own sexual, soulful soliloquy, higher pitched than Celestine's but just as intoxicating. The witch squirted, and both men came again.

"It is hard to decide who is sluttier," Harry said.

"Indeed," the Beast agreed. "Perhaps we should fuck them again."

"A very good idea."

Red smiled as she was Beast-and-wand fucked once more. Her furry companion and her headless one were becoming fast friends over their mutual admiration of the two female sluts in their possession. Red was proud her nymphomania could bring people together. And Celestine was no slouch either. Red greatly admired the older woman's sexual prowess. She'd be her assistant witch slut anytime.

The two couples made love all over the room, eventually collapsing on the bed, Red on top of the Beast and Celestine on top of Harry.

"Does the wand still have to be in my butt?" Red asked.

"Don't be silly," Celestine admonished her. "You should always have something in your ass."

"Oh, right. Okay!" Red wiggled around, making the wand and the Beast's cock massage her insides.

"While that was most enjoyable," her lover said. "I still need to break the curse put upon me."

"So do I," Harry echoed.

"Oh my goddess," Red exclaimed. "I got so caught up in the fucking I forgot to tell you. We brought the rose from the Beast's castle. The one that's supposed to cure any curse."

Harry's head was on the pillow above his body. His eyes lit up. "That's wonderful. Red, I'm in your debt."

"Just give me a good ass ramming, and we'll call it even."

"But I wanted to do that," the Beast objected.

"You can both do it. But, um, not at the same time. You're both too huge for me to take at once."

The Beast and Harry's penises swelled with pride at Red's compliment. Which felt great in both Red and Celestine's pussies.

"Perhaps the rose will provide a clue to curing the Beast as well," Celestine suggested.

"That would be most welcome, but the witch who cursed me said it could cure curses except the one afflicting me."

"Perhaps. But, remember, witches can't be trusted. I used to be a very sneaky witch."

The Beast clasped Red's hips in excitement. "I would be most appreciative of anything you can do."

"Great!" Red exclaimed. "We can cure the curses and then fuck all day and night!"

None of them objected to that plan.

Except the two people who burst into the room.

A man and woman, both around Red's age, stood in the doorway, armed with a sword and crossbow.

"We're Hansel and Gretel," the man said.

"Monster hunters!" his companion added, aiming her bow at the Beast.

Red's eyes went wide.

Well, fuck.

Little Red Riding Slut is a Kindle Vella Series with New Episodes Released Weekly! This book contains Episodes 16-34. Check out new sexy adventures beyond the events of this book at the Little Red Riding Slut Kindle Vella page or on your Android or iPhone.

Fully Nude and Erotic Covers are available on my Patreon page. You can get Nude and Sex Covers of this and other books as well as almost one hundred naked/erotic pictures of my characters. Visit Patreon.com/RileyRoseErotica to check them out!

More Fun and Sexy Books

Remy and the Sex Monsters
Remy Alvarez loves science-fiction and the paranormal. She just didn't expect to be living it. Somehow she finds herself running into all manner of creatures who want to explore every inch of her sexy human body: aliens, sasquatch, horny mad scientists, and more! If they exist, Remy winds up finding them, fully naked and fully ready to be probed! Read her sexy adventures on Kindle Vella!

Sexy Time Cop: Cowgirl and Pirate Sluts
Riley Shu is a Time Cop, stopping criminals from altering the timeline and having sex with the hottest men and women in history! She has to save Wyatt Earp and Doc Holliday in the Old West by being a kinky cowgirl and then it's off to the Caribbean and the Golden Age of Piracy for some submissive shenanigans with Anne Bonny! Will Riley's sexy antics change the timeline? Find out in Sexy Time Cop!

Submissive Princess: Royal Slut
Princess Aaylani is the most beautiful princess in the Seven Queendoms. To avert a war, she must marry Queen Jaiyanna of the neighboring nation of Sosha, a woman known for her kinky domination of her partners. With the help of her handmaiden and best friend Misty, will Aaylani be ready for to become the ultimate submissive princess?

Sexy Tentacles
Kione Ali is an adventurous treasure hunter, always looking to find the next big score. When she gets a clue to Blackbeard's treasure in Barbados, she can't pass up the opportunity to score the notorious pirate's booty. But she never expected to find a tentacle creature with the treasure, one that wants to pleasure Kione in every way possible and tie her up like the submissive sex object she is. Will Kione give in to her kinky curiosity to have tentacle sex? Will she let it explore every inch of her caverns? Find out in this sexy, sensual, tentacle adventure!

Visit RileyRoseErotica.com to get a Free eBook and check out more of my sexy books!

E-mail: Riley@RileyRoseErotica.com

Facebook: RileyRoseErotica
Twitter: @RileyRoserotica
Instagram: @RileyRoseErotica

About the Author

Riley Rose writes comedic, sexy stories featuring fun-loving female protagonists who love taking their clothes off. Discover sexy sci-fi, fantasy, and action/adventure worlds in over forty books and Kindle Vella stories, featuring naughty witches, frisky fairy tale characters, sex-obsessed robots, and titillating tentacles. You'll find fun, friendship, and a ton of submissive sex in Riley's books. Join the sexy shenanigans! Find out more at RileyRoseErotica.com.

Printed in Great Britain
by Amazon